The Secon

- a string quartet novella -

by Peter Neville

*a string quartet novella,
dedicated to everyone
who has ever played string chamber music*

- - Sold in aid of Benslow Music - -

The Second Cello

Peter Neville © 2017
revised 2019

All characters set in the present are fictional, and no resemblance is intended to any existing person.

All rights reserved. No part of this publication may be reproduced, stored in a retrieval system or transmitted in any form or by any means electronic, mechanical, photocopying or otherwise without the prior permission in writing of the author.

The right of Peter Neville to be identified as the author of this work is asserted under the Copyright, Designs & Patents Act 1988.

- *This paperback: available from **www.lulu.com***
- *Downloadable version: available from **www.lulu.com***
- *Paperback and e-reader/Kindle versions: also available from **www.Amazon.co.uk***

ISBN 978-0-244-33692-9

CONTENTS

Chapter		*page*
1	Commissioning	1
2	Dispersal	18
3	Charles	22
4	Beatrice	31
5	Donald and the trio	50
6	Quartet	89
7	Trout	102
8	Schubert Op163	116
9	Performance	127
10	Finale	138

1. Commissioning

He had worked with feverish inspiration, as a man possessed, starting just days after he received the order. He had put all his skill, everything he knew, into making this quartet of instruments. And indeed, the two violins, the viola and the cello were the best he had ever made. They were all from the same log, with the grain of the wood carefully matched.

With pride, he had labelled each of them:

> **MATTHEW HARDIE**
> **Edinburgh, 1811**

And yet, it had all come about quite unexpectedly.

One cold and windy morning, in his cramped premises in a hollow at the foot of Calton Hill, he had been rehairing a bow in his workshop when he heard his shop door being opened. He had been starting to accept orders for cheaper instruments, using plainer timber, anything to put food on the table, and had few expectations when he went to see who had come.

"Oh, good morning, Andrew," said Matthew, "How nice to see you. Business has been very slow lately – it's all these cheap imported German fiddles. Huh, I almost think I should go back to the cabinet-making I used to do. But, oh, sorry, perhaps this a social call? About the Society?"

"Well, yes and no."

They fell into easy conversation. They were both trustees of the Edinburgh Philosophical Society, and both were constantly being invited, for their wide learning and well-informed conversation, to all the city grandees' social events.

They reminisced about the great days of the Society, when their speakers had included Adam Smith, Robert Burns and Joseph Black all in the same season.

"Do you remember that time when James Hutton gave his lecture?" said Andrew. "His family are still farming just along the coast from me. He'd been studying the rocks on the coast and worked out that they must be older than the Bible said. The kirk were furious, but they couldn't prove he was wrong."

"What's gone wrong with Edinburgh?" Matthew mused, "All those great minds. We led the world. Where's that gone? Why, even the Musical Society closed down, what, twelve years ago, and it was good business for me - all the string players came to me for their instruments and repairs. I even had apprentices then."

"Ah, well, that's because everyone knew you're the best. And that's why I'm here."

Apart from being a trustee of the Philosophical Society alongside Matthew, Andrew Darroch was a successful East Lothians farmer. His soil yielded two harvests a year and he had enjoyed high crop prices for several years. His four daughters were promising young string players, playing recitals to gatherings of neighbours and in assembly rooms. He could now afford a worthy quartet of instruments for them.

Matthew Hardie had kept back his best piece of wood for just such an opportunity as this. It was a beam from the old Stock Bridge, demolished in favour of a new stone bridge. The wood was well seasoned, probably a century old already, and the fronts of all four instruments - the most visible part and the most important part for quality of tone - would share the same grain.

As he worked on this commission, he was able to put away his dark memories of the not-so-distant past. To think, he'd been so low that the Duchess of Buccleugh had had to put on a fund-raising ball for him. And then his old comrades from the Duke's regiment had clubbed together to set him up again with tools and material, including the wood from that old bridge.

At last, this prestigious commission, using this very wood, might be a turning point. The instruments he was making would be widely heard by discerning people and would be his best advertisement. He'd been renting this damp hole in Low Calton long enough - he would move back to the Royal Mile, as a public mark of his change in fortune.

As Matthew Hardie admired his finished work, these four exquisitely matched instruments, he idly wondered how long they would be played and how long he would be remembered for having made them. After all, it was barely a hundred years ago that these instruments had finally superseded the viol family, and who knows what new instruments might be coming along in their turn to displace the violin family.

"Tom," he shouted to his young son, "find a messenger – I need to tell Mr Darroch that his instruments are ready. And he needs to know our new address."

"Oh, this is a splendid shop," said Andrew when he arrived a few days later with his carter. "It's so much better than where you were, down at Low Calton. But do I remember you were in the Royal Mile once before?"

"Indeed I was, but it was so expensive it got me into debt and they threw me into jail for it – I had to be more careful with money after that. Debtors' prison was dreadful but, well, I could carry on making in there, to pay it off, and no whisky to distract me."

"Well," said Andrew, "I hope it doesn't happen to you again."

"Which, the debt or the prison? Or the whisky?"

"Good heavens, man," exclaimed Andrew, "please none of them!"

"Quite right, this time will be different. I owe it to all my friends and comrades who helped me out, back then. But come round the back and see your new instruments."

At his first glance, Andrew's jaw dropped at the understated elegance, the beautiful proportions, the unobtrusive light stain, the carefully matched grain, the even varnish.

"Oh, Matthew! What can I say? Here's your guineas." He counted out the gold coins, and added two more.

The girls squealed with delight as their father returned home with the cart, well-padded with hay, containing their four new instruments packed in heavy wooden cases. A servant helped the carter to unload them.

"What shall we play?" asked Isobel, his eldest, and without waiting for an answer, she suggested picking one from the latest Haydn quartets in their collection, the Erdödy set. They had worked hard to master these on their old instruments. "Oh, father," asked Isobel, almost as an afterthought, "have you any newer quartets by Haydn?"

"No, I told you, we can't get any more of his music. I checked with Longman Clementi in London, yes, the people who published the newest ones you have, and they wrote back to me saying that Napoleon is still not allowing anything out of Vienna."

Isobel had to accept this. Her three younger sisters gathered round, tuned up their new instruments, slightly flat so as not to overstress the instruments. Isobel, who always 'led,' nodded, and they started the fourth Erdödy quartet by Haydn, the "Sunrise."

"We could try something harder," suggested Isobel at the end of the first movement. "What about the sixth of these, yes the one at the end of book?"

"Oh no," moaned her first-violin sister. "That's the one that sounds as if the music had been through a mincer, all bits and pieces of phrases. And I've hundreds of notes to play in it."

"Well, just one movement, then," conceded Isobel.

At the end of the first movement, they felt it had gone unusually well, and agreed to try the second.

And then the third.

And then the last.

At the end, they looked at each other, bemused. "We *did* it," said the first violinist.

"Well, we can't leave it there," declared Isobel. "Do you remember that set of three new quartets that Father got us? Yes, the ones by that new revolutionary composer. Yes, the ones we gave up because we couldn't make sense of them?"

"Oh yes, I remember now," replied one of her sisters sheepishly, "all the parts were hard, like nothing we'd seen before."

"Ah! Here they are!" shouted Isobel in triumph, as she pulled out a set of three quartets labelled Beethoven Opus 18. "After that Haydn, I'm sure we can play *anything* on these new instruments."

Andrew, sitting in his library, had never heard the last Erdödy quartet played through with such confidence and musicality. And now his daughters were tackling the Beethoven, he heard a shaky but still extraordinary quartet beginning to take shape.

The girls were so absorbed they would not stop for their meal. Their next run-through revealed a masterwork played with gripping ensemble and interplay between the parts. Andrew felt he had a sensation on his hands. His wife added that if the girls would only agree to wear her choice of dress, they would win over everyone everywhere.

And they did.

At the end of yet another triumphant and well-attended performance, in the drawing room of a near-neighbour, a servant was just loading the cello case into the boot under the coachman's seat when the horses took fright and bolted. After some yards, the cello case tumbled out onto the stone roadway with a sickening crunch and then rolled over a few times under its forward momentum, before coming to rest.

Matthew watched with shock as the wrecked case was carefully carried into his shop.

Andrew stuttered, "We thought it best not to open the case ourselves..., we thought..., and the quartet were sounding just heavenly..."

"Please, just me look in peace."

Matthew levered off the splintered front of the case. Inside was a thoroughly smashed cello. Just sorting the smithereens into the right order to put it together, if that were even possible, would take weeks. He choked to see his loving work reduced to this wreckage.

After a few moments, his practical side re-asserted itself. Andrew would need a loan cello at once, sooner than he could possibly repair this one or make a replacement.

"Tom," he shouted to his son, "go round to David Stirrat and tell him Mr Darroch needs to borrow his best cello, because I don't have one in stock that's good enough. Yes, you remember, he's just moved into the Fleshmarket. Yes, nine storeys up. You lazy... when I was your age..."

Surprisingly quickly, Tom reappeared carrying a cello case, with David Stirrat walking alongside. Tom put the case down with a sigh of

10

relief and ran off upstairs. While Andrew Darroch looked at David's cello, David said to Matthew Hardie, "Yes, I'm always glad to help you out. Any odd bits of work you want me to do... I need to get established here as a maker, they don't know me here yet, like they did in Ayrshire. Well, all right, that can be my hire fee for lending out my cello, the tonewood from Andrew's smashed instrument. Although, thinking about it, wouldn't you want to keep the wreckage for Tom, for him to rebuild it, learn his craft?"

"No, I can't make up my mind about Tom. I'd like him to take up making. But he's only a boy, hasn't the right temperament. Come to that, nor has my other son."

Andrew coughed politely, to remind the two makers that he was still there. "Right," he said, "I'll be proud to borrow Mr Stirrat's cello here, although, hmm, maybe it's just slightly large for my eldest. Matthew, I think your standard pattern of cello is perhaps just a fraction smaller?"

"No, my standard isn't, but as the set was for your girls, I made the cello to ladies'-size."

"Well, I've decided now, please make a replacement. Here's my deposit money." He laid out gold coins from his purse. "No offence meant, Mr Stirrat, I'm sure your instruments are excellent, but as Matthew made me a set of four, I want to keep it that all four are by the same maker, even if they're not the matched set they once were."

Andrew's daughters continued to play to music societies and at gatherings of friends, but their ensemble sound had lost its sheen. The girls all knew this was not their playing, which was getting better all the time as they continued to study and practise and as they themselves were still growing. Isobel, not wishing to upset her father, said nothing to him, except to praise the Stirrat cello for making her open her left hand more fully. She said nothing of the extra physical effort it took to play.

Matthew had meanwhile gone off gloomily to inspect his stock of wood. While the money was always useful, he saw this as just a job of work rather than a labour of love. But, as he perused his wood, his heart speeded up. Yes, he still had part of the original plank from the old Stock Bridge, and yes, he could probably still match the grain to Andrew's remaining three instruments.

And so, a few months later, Andrew Darroch was back in the Royal Mile to collect his replacement cello.

"It's as near a duplicate as I could manage," Matthew Hardie explained. "You see, it was from memory – I couldn't face going round to David Stirrat's to look at what's left of the original, you'll understand, I hope." He went to a cupboard behind the counter. "And here it is."

"Oh!" exclaimed Andrew at his first glance, "I think it looks wonderful, yes, really wonderful. Let me pay you now. Oh, and let me return my loan cello." He whistled outside for his carter to bring the Stirrat cello into the shop.

"Between you and me," he continued, "and for goodness sake don't tell Mr Stirrat, I don't think my Isobel got on with his cello. It was just too big, too heavy for her, it seemed hard work for her to play it."

"Why, did she say all that to you?" asked Matthew, eager for any informed feedback on his, and others', instruments.

"No. Not a word. She's so loyal. But I could tell."

A few weeks later, Andrew Darroch invited Matthew Hardie to the daughters' next concert. This would be Matthew's first chance to hear these four instruments of his together, even though they were, strictly, not a set. The girls were performing an ambitious programme: a string quartet by Boccherini, and one of the string quartets written by Mozart for the King of Prussia. Boccherini and the King of Prussia were both fine cellists, and the cello parts of the quartets reflected this. Matthew therefore wondered whether Isobel had been wise to set herself such a challenge. He little knew how hard Andrew had tried to dissuade Isobel.

The girls entered, elegantly dressed, as their mother wished, in matching high-waisted cream muslin dresses, being very much the style of the time. Matthew noticed how the girls were each at their own stage of becoming young women, and how fetching this style looked on them. But would their playing match their appearance?

Matthew could not credit his ears. Isobel's showpiece passages were as close to perfection as he'd ever heard, and her sisters were maintaining a tight even ensemble. But what surprised him even more is how the tedious hours of drudgery in his workshop had paid off. The four instruments blended to sound as one, even though the low pitch and extra resonance of cellos meant they never usually blended quite as well into a quartet ensemble.

A new Music Circle had just been formed, and Matthew decided to ask whether Andrew's quartet could be invited to perform at one of the its concerts. There could not be a better advertisement for his instruments.

Hearing nothing in reply from Andrew for some time, Matthew decided to ask him at the next meeting of the Philosophical Society, where Dugald Stewart was to lecture on the Scottish Enlightenment.

But before that date came round, a well-dressed stranger came into Matthew's shop and asked, "Am I in the right place, sir? Can you kindly recall, sir, did you make a set of instruments for Mr Andrew Darroch?"

"Why, yes," Matthew answered, "I remember them very well, they are among my finest work. Are you by any chance wishing me to make a similar set for you?"

"Alas no," laughed the stranger ruefully, "there is no musical ability in my branch of the family. I am Mr Darroch's cousin, and I come with sad news. Before he left, he gave me a list of his close and trusted friends to be informed."

"Left? Informed? What's happened?"

"He said I could trust you. Since Napoleon was defeated, there has been a crash in corn prices. Mr Darroch's tenants cannot pay him their rent. He cannot sell his own crops for even the cost of the wages to harvest them. He cannot pay his debts. He has fled to Canada with his wife and daughters, leaving me to wind down his affairs as best I can."

"Oh, this is dreadful news," Matthew responded. "I rated him as a good friend, not just a client. We got on well together. Hm. Can I help in any way? Not money, but anything else?"

"Thank you, maybe you can. Can you buy back his daughters' instruments?"

"Oh dear, I'm sorry, that would stretch me too much. But if you need cash in a hurry for Mr Darroch's benefit, I suggest you take them to an auction house."

2. *Dispersal*

Lord Shetland emerged from the Court of Session building. His last case before the vacation had been cancelled, and the next boat to take him back home to the Shetlands would not sail from Leith until the following morning's tide. With all this unexpected time on his hands, he ambled the streets aimlessly until he noticed the flag flying outside the city's main auction rooms, showing that a sale was in progress.

To pass the time, he wandered in. He saw some uninteresting lots of household furniture go under the hammer for small sums. He was about to leave when some silver tableware came up. He looked but decided not to bid for any of it and was again about to leave, when two violins came up. He remembered how his fiddler back home was having trouble with his instrument, and not playing the reels with his normal aplomb.

"Excuse me," shouted Lord Shetland across the auction room, "I might bid, if you let me hear these being played."

"You should have come to the viewing," replied the auctioneer in irritation.

"I couldn't, I'm a..." He trailed off, not wanting to reveal he was one of Scotland's most senior judges.

The auctioneer started the bidding. Two bidders were interested at the start, but soon one shook his head.

"Going to the gentleman in grey for a bid of..." announced the auctioneer, raising his hammer.

"No!" shouted the losing bidder, seeing a chance to exact revenge on his richer rival, "I'll play it to this stranger, he might bid you higher, why not?"

Before anyone could intervene, the losing bidder had grabbed the violin, took the bow which was included in the lot, and started to play a strathspey.

That was exactly the sound Lord Shetland wanted to hear from his own fiddler. He bid double the last bid, which silenced the auction room. After completing the purchase formalities, he walked weakly out of the auction rooms, shocked by his impulsiveness in having suddenly become the owner of an expensive violin he couldn't himself play.

The auctioneer had been canny in keeping back the viola and cello for a future sale, and now, on the spur of the moment, he withdrew the second violin, ignoring the grumbling of the two men who had just been outbid.

The story of the bidding war for the 'Shetland' violin soon got about, and, just as the auctioneer had intended, at the next sale the second violin fetched even more than the Shetland violin. Andrew Darroch's debts were starting to be cleared.

But the viola and the cello did not attract serious interest, and so the auctioneer took them to a generalist musical instrument dealer, and negotiated a price.

Almost at once, the cello caught the eye of a jobbing instrument-maker/repairer named Joseph Meall, who would come in, as required, to do work for the dealer. Seeing a nefarious opportunity, Joseph bought the cello direct off the dealer, intending to remove the Hardie label and put it into his own inferior cello, which he would then sell at a 'Hardie' price. He would then put one of his own labels into the Hardie cello, to inflate his own reputation as a maker.

3. Charles

Within a few weeks, the viola was bought by a young university student from England. He had wanted to study music but his parents persuaded him to take a university degree in medicine. They were quite prepared to meet the extra expense of his studying in Scotland, because his father had trod the same path before him, the English universities being closed to them as Nonconformists. His father had thus acquired contacts in Edinburgh, and wrote his son letters of introduction in case of need.

The son applied himself diligently to his medical studies, but also sought out the university musical scene, where his fellow students had mentioned the name of Matthew Hardie as an excellent contemporary maker. When he spotted this viola at the dealer's, he was therefore delighted to acquire a well-played-in Matthew Hardie for less than its cost new.

In course of time he graduated, and family tradition would have required him to join his father's medical practice. However, during his time as a student, Edinburgh's musical life was starting to revive with the influx of wealthy citizens to the developing New Town. The son found he had a blossoming spare-time musical career, and was torn between his father's practice and the concert platform.

His father took it well, but cautioned his son just how risky the musical profession was, especially for a player of such a 'Cinderella' instrument as the viola. He therefore organised a part-time placement for his son at one of his medical contacts in Edinburgh, a compromise which the son gratefully accepted.

At a time when the viola was regarded as merely a tiresome necessity in orchestras and string quartets, with virtually no solo repertoire, he managed to forge a career playing what little there was – the two Stamitz concertos, the Telemann concerto and sonata, and Mozart's Sinfonia Concertante. His masterstroke was to arrange for advance copies of Schubert's string quartets to be sent to him as soon as completed and ahead of official publication; using this advantage, he secured a contract with the Music Circle to present each quartet as an Edinburgh premiere. He continued this dual musical/medical career in Edinburgh until his father's retirement, when he moved back to England to run the family medical practice.

His musical success became something of a family legend, and his viola was kept in the family and handed down through the generations, even though nobody played it any more.

Six generations on, the son of the family (called Charles as in all previous generations), was a highly-regarded medic (of course), and in addition was a highly capable pianist. However, he also enjoyed the sociability of orchestral playing, and therefore persisted as a passable (but not outstanding) hobby violinist on his passable (but not outstanding) violin, a familiar sight in the back desk of the second-violin sections of local amateur orchestras.

When Charles inherited the viola, his musically knowledgeable wife reminded him – repeatedly – that orchestras and groups were constantly complaining about the shortage of viola players. So, to humour her, he had the viola tidied up and restrung, and tentatively tried it out. He suddenly found, having strong arms and long fingers, that he had an instrument which suited his physique much better.

While struggling to master the alto clef, he was also, without consciously realising it, waking up this long-neglected viola. Its response took him by surprise. Soon, it was answering eagerly to his touch, like a girl hungry for her lover's kisses. Really, Charles, he admonished himself, you're a happily married man and a cool-headed medic, what are you thinking, conjuring up such images in your mind.

The awakening of the viola and his confidence in the alto clef seemed to come together at the same time, in his first orchestral concert as a viola player. In the final rehearsal on the afternoon of the concert, in Glazunov's Violin Concerto he had started to notice that, at a tempo change coinciding with a return of key to three sharps, the violas had a striking few bars of tune in unison with the bassoons.

At the concert, he did not let his wife's presence near the front distract him, but concentrated on being, even if new to the role, a solid member of the viola section. Thus he sensed, when approaching this tempo change in the concert, that the violas in front of him had become disoriented by the preceding music in five flats. With the ability that came with his medical experience to re-prioritise instantly for the greater good, he stopped trying to play in that thankless key but concentrated on keeping his place. At the key change to three sharps, he sensed some fumbling in the bassoons, possibly a muffed page turn (the orchestral parts were in deplorable condition), but he knew he was bang-on in the right place and powered out the tune from the back desk. His colleagues followed his lead and the moment was saved.

As the concerto neared its end, there was an animando passage during one of the few rests for the concerto soloist. In rehearsals, he had noticed that the violas had a rhythmic semiquaver figure by themselves at this point, governing the acceleration of the music and locking the harmonic relationship of the other slower-moving parts.

Now that it was the real concert performance, he wondered whether concert nerves might afflict his colleagues. His back-desk view of the conductor was too intermittent for him to risk reading the beat upon reaching this animando, so he decisively pushed out the semiquavers at the same rate of acceleration as at rehearsal. Well, he had nothing to lose, he was only a back-desk viola on his first concert in the section. It seemed to have worked, everyone was following him, the music was continuing under its own momentum and the soloist then came in quite happily. He was starting to enjoy this back-seat driving.

At the interval, the violas huddled together backstage over their coffees. After a short silence, the principal viola spoke:

"Charles, that was hardly in the spirit of sectional discipline, was it? But I have to hand it to you, you came in when we were stuck. Twice."

"Yes, there's something odd about the lighting," said another player, "those extra lights they put in just for the concert, you're watching the conductor OK, then he moves an inch and you lose him in the glare. It's very offputting."

"Especially to viola players," said a voice.

Everyone looked round sharply, but relaxed when they saw it was one of their own, speaking in a put-on voice.

"It's worse nearer the front. On a back desk, it's probably not so bad."

The conversation degenerated into the usual banter about it being better to ignore the conductor at all times, giving Charles the chance to dash round to the auditorium and catch up with his wife for a few moments before he returned backstage.

There, it was soon time for the musicians to line up, ready to march onto the stage in order, with the leader and conductor coming on last. This orderly entrance looked impressive, or would do, if it weren't for the percussionists and double bassists, who never thought it applied to them and would shamble on early, in ragged disorder, just when they felt like it.

"Oh," said a percussionist, when once tackled about it, "we have to come on early, to tune the timps. It's impossible once the rest of the orchestra is in and tuning up."

"And," added a bass player, "the orchestra always use the bass section area as their M1 for getting to their places. We have to be there first, holding our basses upright, to stop them being knocked over and trampled."

"So, who would notice if they were?" asked a flautist.

The one work after the interval was Beethoven's 5th Symphony. The first movement went well, having been extensively rehearsed as it was so well known.

The second movement opens in 4 flats – a key which Charles noticed was mercifully easier on the viola than the violin – with an eight-bar 3/8 passage in same-octave unison with the cellos, with bass accompaniment.

There had been a tendency in rehearsal to leave this pretty much to the cellos, with their superior projection, but, sitting now on the concert platform, Charles decided otherwise. He was on a roll. The considered decisiveness that made him a successful A&E consultant was turning out to be equally useful on the back desk of the violas. Charles considered that Beethoven would not have specified for the violas to join the cellos unless he had wanted the different tonal blend that violas could contribute.

So, he acted accordingly. He enunciated the tune with bold confidence, rather more strongly than the official dynamic marking. And why not, he thought, dynamics had to be taken in context, and if this was the statement of the theme, then it should be played for the audience to hear. As far as he could tell from his back-desk position, the tone quality of the theme was different from before, more smooth and rounded from the newly rebalanced blend between cellos and violas.

No time to congratulate himself as, fifteen bars later, the violas would lead off with a choppy semiquaver arpeggiated accompaniment figure, joined later by the violins an octave higher. Yes, play it out, he thought, especially if my front desk are being blinded by the lights.

Another twelve bars later, a flowing semiquaver melody in same-octave unison with the cellos. Then in a few moments, a violas-only hemi-demi-semiquaver accompaniment figure. And so it went on. This was viola heaven.

It was this occasion that inspired him to concentrate on the viola, and he went on to become an outstanding player in his county.

4. Beatrice

Beatrice was a music graduate who, for her day job, had had to make a career outside music, in her case as an optician's assistant near her home in the London's outer commuterland. As a sideline, she had started to take piano and violin pupils, and over the years had built up quite a practice.

Meanwhile, she had joined the Chiltern Philharmonia, an amateur orchestra originally founded by a group of music teachers. Because of its quality, it drew a nucleus of capable players from a wide area. As Beatrice's ability became recognised, she began to be moved up the ranks of the second-violin section.

At a Chilterns Phil rehearsal one day, at the coffee break, the Principal second violinist called the section together.

"The Leader's been let down by one of his First violins and has asked one of us to cross over. Any takers? No? Well, I'm not really surprised, it takes a particular temperament to be a good Second violin. Hm, you're a lovely section and I don't really want to leave you, but it looks like it'll have to be me, then. So, now you'll need a new Principal. I'm wondering whether…"

"We want Beatrice," shouted one, and the others nodded.

"Good," replied the outgoing Principal, "I'm glad that's settled – I'd have picked her too, except it would have been none of my business now. Congratulations, Beatrice, and the best of luck!"

Resuming after the coffee break, she moved to her new seat. She heard some whispered negotiations behind her, as those desks who didn't want to be split up invited players from behind to leapfrog them to ensure two to each desk. The new seating agreed, the second violinists shuffled up accordingly.

Settled now in her seat, Beatrice looked round wonderingly at her section, who looked expectantly back.

There they all were, dear old Oswald, who, for eyesight reasons, preferred to sit by himself with his own music stand, to the side of the main block of second violin desks.

Then lovely Marmaduke at the back, who was always about a beat behind and had a permanent expression of puzzlement on his face. And his inseparable desk partner Enid, who tried so hard but, on page-turning, would pull the music off their music stand sending it cascading onto the floor. And there was Portia, a good player if only she could count her rests more accurately. Not to mention Cedric and Rosie and the others and their foibles...

She loved them all, every one. They were *her* section. *She* would look after them. She looked at them, and smiled. They smiled back.

She nodded, then turned to face the conductor, ready for the downbeat.

By the end of the rehearsal, she was quite exhausted from the pressure of having to play her part not only note-perfectly and with the correct bowing, but also without fluffs or hesitations, encouraging her section by positive body language and gestures, in short really *leading* her section by example.

This is when she began to curse her college violin, which she had owned from new and which she had adored. It was beginning to show its limitations, and would let her down in embarrassing ways, such as by splitting a note without warning in the middle of an obbligato solo. She discussed this with her new co-principal desk partner.

"I'd say you've outgrown your fiddle. You need a better one now, especially now you're in the sectional hot-seat."

"But I *couldn't*! I gave this violin its voice, it's *my* voice, I brought it to life from new, I'm the only person who's ever played it in its whole life, I couldn't be so disloyal, it would feel like I'm betraying it, being unfaithful to it…"

"Do it! I'm telling you! You're sitting on the right-hand side of this desk because you're better than I am, and you deserve to be there. But now you're there, you owe it to the section, the section is looking to you for leadership. Have you led a section before? No, I thought not. Well, you need a violin befitting."

"But I *can't;* it would feel so disloyal, I would feel dirty, I…"

"All right, keep that violin, keep it for teaching, keep it for the rough stuff like Shostakovitch symphonies or jazzy shows."

"But then I'll lose the chance to use its trade-in value."

"Any excuse!"

A few months after this conversation, the Chiltern Philharmonic planned to put on a concert featuring two strings-only pieces, namely Elgar's *Introduction & Allegro* and the Vaughan Williams *Fantasia on a Theme by Thomas Tallis*.

The *Fantasia* is written for a solo string quartet plus a standard string orchestra, with an additional miniature (nine-piece) string orchestra sitting well apart from the others. The Chiltern Philharmonic's committee had considered hiring-in a top professional string quartet to play the challenging solo string quartet music, but ran into opposition from the membership. The matter was finally settled when the Hon. Treasurer ruled out the idea as too costly, although he conceded that it would still be necessary to import a few semi-professional string extras from around the county and beyond, to ensure full capability in all parts of this 14-line score.

Being keen for the strings-only pieces to be a success, the string players had practised their parts thoroughly. Accordingly, the rehearsals went well, and the afternoon-of-the-concert rehearsal went very well. This included some of the tricky corners, notably in the Elgar, where, in a slow-up in the Allegro, the principal viola plays solo an isolated group of four semiquavers, followed a beat later by the same for principal second violin, followed again a beat later by the same for principal cello, linking then to a recollection of an earlier theme.

In the concert, when the music reached this tricky corner, Beatrice, as principal second violin, correctly waited for one beat after Simon, the principal viola, played his semiquavers on viola, and then...

Some minute change in the humidity affecting the bow-hair, some fractional build-up of rosin on the string, who knows, Beatrice split her first note... and the next three didn't speak at all, as the string refused to answer to the bow.

The principal cellist, who had to follow her a beat later, was momentarily disoriented but luckily collected his wits in time for the music to hold together.

During the applause at the end of the piece, Beatrice's co-principal tactfully said nothing, but just patted her in sympathetic consolation.

She was dreading the *Fantasia* after the interval. As second violin of the solo quartet, she didn't have a particularly exposed part, but still didn't want to let the others down through her violin failing to respond to her bow.

The interval seemed to drag on for ages, while the orchestra seating was being re-arranged into the three ensembles required in the Fantasia. Beatrice spent the time usefully, cleaning her strings to remove build-up of old rosin and checking her bow. The members of her section came up to wish her well in her solo quartet position in the *Fantasia,* and she thanked them politely. In the re-arranged seating, her co-principal would be sitting elsewhere, leading the second violins in the main string orchestra.

Her violin behaved itself throughout the introduction and development of the *Fantasia,* and she began to enjoy the sonorous antiphonal writing. At the close of the development section, all instruments fall silent except the solo viola, with a melody derived from part of the original theme. She admired Simon's fluent playing of this passage.

The first violin then repeats the viola solo, joined soon by the viola engaging in an elaborate counterpoint. This was Beatrice's signal to concentrate, as she herself would soon have a few bars in the limelight. Her heart was in her mouth, but she was in luck for now - her violin obeyed her.

And from here on to the end, she mostly had other parts doubling her, somewhere or other in the texture. She was safe. But it had been nerve-wracking, and through no fault of her own. She couldn't ever go through all that again. She knew what her co-principal would have said if he could have read her thoughts.

The very next morning, she was online, looking up auction houses for their forthcoming musical-instrument sales dates. Then she made a list of possible dealers.

At the next rehearsal, she asked her co-principal his advice.

"Well, dealers will look after you, patch your violin up if there's some defect, they want to keep a good reputation. But auction houses, well, you're swimming alone with the sharks."

"Hmm, how much would I pay for the comfort blanket of buying from a dealer?"

"Well, see it from his point of view. He puts his money on the line, whether it's part-exchange or he's buying direct. So the stock sits in his shop for maybe years, and he's paying staff and rent all the while. You guess."

"OK, I don't have money to burn, it has to be an auction – I'll take the chance."

"Attagirl! You'll save thousands for taking the risk. Oh, and don't forget, they add commission and all sorts to the hammer price, so bear that in mind that when you're working out how high to bid."

While waiting for the next big London auction, she haunted dealerships, tried out their stock, and noted the price-tags. As she played more and more different violins, her fingers began to learn to estimate value. The dealers seemed quite relaxed about her visits even when she showed no obvious intention of buying.

"Why do you just let me come in, a complete stranger, and not mind me playing all your valuable stock?"

"Ah, you might find *the* violin of your dreams. And while you're looking for it, you're keeping our stock in a played-in condition – very important, that. Oh, and the sound of a good instrument being tried out in the back room – customers in the front shop like to hear it, it's good for business. You come in as much as you like!"

Soon the central-London auction houses' next catalogues came online, but Beatrice couldn't see anything listed in the first one that stood out. Even when she went to the viewing, she was disappointed.

She asked an attendant, "I thought you'd have a wider variety here, to view. Wouldn't all you auction houses be better to spread your dates out more? Your sale is the very day before the Savoy's!"

"Oh, that's deliberate, madam, we all co-ordinate our dates. It's for the convenience of overseas buyers – they come to London and can attend all the important viewings and sales in just one visit."

The Savoy list did have one intriguing item; she had heard of Italian, German, French, English violins of course, but a *Scottish* violin? Having been disappointed in her first viewing, she went the next day to the Savoy's viewing more in curiosity than hope.

She soon found the Scottish violin.

It was unimpressive to look at. The varnish was muted, even dull. The woodgrain was plain, and the curves were neither flamboyant nor elegant, just subdued.

Well, she had selected it from the catalogue and had made the journey here – she might as well try it. Determined not to like it, she picked it up and folded her scarf to make an improvised chin rest. Then she picked up a bow which was also for sale. She suddenly noticed that nobody was playing any of the instruments, nor, it now struck her, had anyone played at the other viewing yesterday.

Somewhat self-consciously, and suffering from the lack of a shoulder rest, she played a few scales and passages, while everyone else was continuing to evaluate the instruments purely by sight.

Her fingers were telling her that the auction-house's lower-end estimate was about right. The violin spoke reliably and easily, which she liked, but more softly than she would have wished.

She asked a man viewing bows at the next table to play the violin while she went to the opposite corner of the room. Without shoulder or chin rest, he elected to hold it dancing-master-style against his upper arm. After a few moments' experimentation, he got it to speak. Though soft, the sound carried well. Yes, she would be more than happy to make that sound.

"How did you know I could play the violin?" asked the man, "and not fitted up either? It was risky of you to ask me, I might be a rival bidder, wanting it for my shop, and now everyone in the room has heard what it can do."

"So, what are you telling me, all these people are dealers, and, what, they just go by the appearance and the name on the label inside?"

"That's about it. Condition doesn't matter to them within reason, they've got workshops to patch up any faults. Private buyers are a minority. Too risky. Put an impulse bid, the instrument turns out to be a pup, all down to you." As an afterthought, he added, "I'm not a dealer, and you're all right, I'm not bidding on that violin, I'm after a bow."

He winked, and then returned to the table with bows which he had been inspecting.

Here was the first instrument she'd seen that she wanted to bid for, but she was terrified of being carried away in the heat of the auction. Better if she could put in a bid without being there. She asked an attendant. Yes, she could do that. She would have to comply with various formalities, and here was the form to fill out. Cautiously, she set her maximum bid at rather below the lower-end estimate.

"Lot 43, hm," said the clerk when Beatrice phoned in, the day after the auction, "let me just check, ah, yes, it did sell, and, let's see, yes, your maximum limit was the successful bid."

Oh dear, she had won her very first auction. At her top limit. She worried she must have overbid.

"Now I've bought it, can you tell me anything about the history of this violin? Who's owned it?"

"I'm sorry madam," replied the clerk, "the seller has asked to remain anonymous."

Anxious to miss as little time as possible from work, she went early, with her spare violin case, shoulder rest and bow, to the auction house, which (she was glad to have discovered) opened at 8am. She was directed downstairs to the cash office, to a part of the building never seen by the millionaires who bid in the sumptuously carpeted and chandeliered rooms upstairs. It was shabby and uninviting down here, which did nothing to help her sense of worry about having overbid.

Having emptied her savings account and received a tatty paper collection chit in return, she walked from the cash office along a cold stone basement passageway to the even shabbier warehouse counter. She shivered, but then cheered up just slightly at the sight of the attendant bringing *her* violin to her. Despite its low-key appearance, she did recognise it, and took it briefly in her hands before packing it carefully in her case. But she was still in a state of 'buyer's remorse', not helped by the feeling, on her complex journey from central London to the outer-suburban opticians where she worked, that she was somehow in the wrong, fighting her way at every change of train against the rush-hour crowds surging into central London. The last stage of her journey out of London, in a near-empty train, seemed to take an eternity.

Arriving at the opticians, she plunged straight into her work and said nothing until the lunch break.

Finding an empty workroom, she got out her new violin, fitted her shoulder rest, tuned the violin, improvised a chin rest, and cautiously played a scale. Then another scale. No weak spots, and an easy and even response. Encouraged, she started Monti's *Czardas*.

As she played the finishing chords, her boss rushed in and shouted "Come out into the front shop. Yes, with your violin, Yes, now!"

There, she saw the customers sitting applauding and wreathed in smiles.

"They thought I'd got a CD on," explained her boss, "and I had to tell them it was you, live."

The Chiltern Philharmonia committee noticed Beatrice's improved sound with her new violin, and, in their tradition of occasionally showcasing their principals as concerto soloists, they decided that she and Simon (the principal viola) should play Mozart's exquisite Sinfonia Concertante for Violin and Viola.

As soon as this had been made definite in the Chiltern Philharmonia's programme for the next season, Simon searched for any upcoming concert which he could attend, featuring the Sinfonia Concertante. So, he was disconcerted to discover that it would be performed by the Chiltern Phil's rivals the Downs Ensemble, in the very same church and only a few weeks before. Not an inspired piece of planning by the Chiltern Phil, he reflected ruefully.

When he went to hear the Downs, once he got over the shock of how chilly the church was, he was pleasantly surprised to see that he knew the viola soloist. It was Charles, and although they hadn't met recently, Simon remembered being impressed by Charles when they had shared a desk for some gala event. Despite the chill, Charles's performance this evening did not disappoint.

Therefore, when practising for the Chiltern Philharmonia concert, Simon was content simply to model his interpretation on Charles's. The concert was heavily promoted and, despite the recent Downs Ensemble concert, advance sales of tickets were healthy.

But just a few days before the concert, Simon fell over a kerb and broke his wrist. Depressed as he was at instantly losing several months'-worth of concerts, shows and weddings, he was sufficiently self-disciplined to appoint deputies for his more important engagements. His first call was to Charles to step in for the Chiltern Philharmonia concert. Most unusually for Charles, he was still free at this short notice. Charles did point out that he didn't think he had ever played with Beatrice, but Simon agreed this would just have to be accepted in this emergency.

As they had had no chance to read through the solo parts together, Charles arranged with Beatrice to meet on the day of the concert in the church, just before the afternoon dress rehearsal. When he arrived, it was even chillier than before, and there was a cacophony of staging being erected, pews moved, and orchestra seating and lights shifted into position.

"You must be Charles," said Beatrice, "and thanks for arriving so promptly. Sorry about the din! Well let's try the bit at..."

Through the cold and all the distractions, they played as one and were astonished how well their instruments sounded together.

"That was good. Tonight might even be OK," said Beatrice. "Actually perhaps you could solve another problem we've got - could you take over our principal viola seat, just for the next few weeks, just until Simon, er..., aah, thank you!"

Once the orchestra had straggled in, the rehearsal was passable but unexciting, as the Chiltern Philharmonia players were an experienced bunch and knew well to save their ultimate efforts for the performance.

The church heating had started to take effect by the evening. The church was full for the concert, and, spurred by the sense of occasion plus the desire to outshine the Downs Ensemble, the orchestra played with extra care and sensitivity. The solo parts intertwined with a rarely heard unity and beauty. It was unforgettable.

Sitting in the audience was Donald, whose firm of actuaries in Scotland had recently transferred him to their London office. It was an important early-career promotion, but the move had still left him lonely and homesick. It could have been worse; while preparing for the move, he had fortunately kept in mind the words of a music teacher of his boyhood: "Keep up your music, because it will help you to meet people all through your life, and they'll always be the *right* people." He remembered the words exactly, because, with the irreverence of a schoolboy, he had laughed at such a sweeping unprovable statement. But the words stuck – he kept up his cello playing to the best standard he could, and had brought his cello with him to England.

At the end of the concert, knowing the players would be too busy packing and clearing up for any lengthy chat about how to join their orchestra, Donald tapped a message on his phone to the orchestra's address published in the programme. Before sending, he revised his message – he deleted his request to attend a rehearsal, saying instead that he wanted to play with Beatrice and Charles. He pressed 'Send'.

5. Donald and the trio

Impressed by his brazen cheek, Beatrice and Charles decided to humour him, and agreed to meet him at the orchestra's rehearsal venue half an hour before the rehearsal time, with every intention of outclassing him and sending him away.

"Let's throw one of the Pleyel trios at him," suggested Beatrice.

"Or, actually my first study is piano, we could throw a piano trio at him."

"Piano? Hm, that's useful to know. I play it too, take pupils, it's a sideline for me, but no, to be fair to this interloper, he's expecting us on violin and viola."

"All right then," said Charles, "but not Pleyel. The *Boccherini* string trios are even flashier and harder for the cello. That'll get rid of him, no argument."

"I've a better idea still," replied Beatrice, "We'll meet him an *hour* before the rehearsal and make him play Mozart's Divertimento with us, all of it, straight through without a break."

"What, K563, his one-and-only string trio? Without warning? It takes nearly all of an hour. You wouldn't, that's cruel."

"Yes, that's exactly the idea."

Although they were indeed better players than he was, he kept up with them, throughout this titanic work, which is both physically and emotionally draining for all three players equally. Though his playing was on the stolid side, he maintained a clarity of tone and instinctive ensemble that surprised all three of them.

"Well," admitted Beatrice, "we didn't know what to expect – we'd never met you, and, I must be honest, at the end of this session, I was fully intending to say, 'Thank you and goodbye'. But after this, I could actually see us playing as a serious trio."

Charles agreed, and added, "Beatrice and I have only just discovered, we both play instruments by Matthew Hardie – you fitted in so well, I'd swear that yours was a Hardie too!"

"Oh, no. Mind you, it *is* Scottish – it's labelled Joseph Meall. I gather he was some obscure repairer in Edinburgh – seems to have known his job all right."

At a Chilterns Philharmonia rehearsal a few weeks later, Charles rushed in. "Beatrice! Donald! Get your diaries, I've just been offered a wedding!"

"You've got a wedding job? How do you make the time, don't you ever work in that hospital of yours?"

"Ah, I'm on a part-time contract, I can decide how many hours I put in. And my colleagues are brilliant if I ask to swap shifts with them. I want to keep a decent work-life balance. Family and music, they keep me sane."

"But there's only three of us, you need another violin surely, for a wedding?"

"No, no, I know the venue, it's very cramped. I told the bride she couldn't have a string quartet because there was only room for a trio. She was fine with that. And remember, we *have* played K563 together, right through, unrehearsed!"

"Ah," said Beatrice, "now here's a bit of luck. An old-folks' home has asked me if I can lay on a musical entertainment..."

"...and," Charles interrupted, "you want to use it as a chance to rehearse the wedding music! Right?"

Donald remained silent.

"Well, Donald?"

"You're established players hereabouts, I've only just come down south, it's not my gig, I can hardly..."

"Yes or no? Try out our programme first at a seniors' knees-up?"

"Well, yes!"

The manageress of the care home was effusive when the trio arrived for the performance, and detailed her staff to help set up the residents' lounge to the trio's requirements.

The residents entered for the performance, most with the help of carers, but some unaided. They paid close attention to the manageress's introduction, and clearly enjoyed the trio's opening offering, which was a set of arrangements (for trio) of wedding-suitable light classics.

Following this set, Charles stood and talked briefly about Mozart's Trio K563, putting it in its musical and historic context and explaining the structure of the music about to be unfolded.

The opening unison minim-paced downward arpeggio was spot-on in tune and time, and the three instruments, as always, sounded like one instrument with three identical voices. This locked the audience's attention, despite their infirmities, throughout the lengthy and complex first movement.

The players then tackled the slow and emotional second movement. Beatrice held her double-stopped chords for Donald's slow rising arpeggio and, despite the cruel change of double-stop, she answered the end of his crotchets with a pulverisingly accurate quaver beat. Later, Charles would have to execute some nasty double-stops of his own, an inevitable feature of four-part harmony written for three instruments. It was small consolation that Mozart himself, who usually took the viola part in his own chamber music compositions, would have played those very notes.

Come the first repeat mark, Donald wrongly assumed that they were omitting that repeat and went straight on to the development section in the implied key of E♭-minor, leading soon to his playing a D♮ against Beatrice's D♭/E♭ double-stop.

This unMozartian discord broke the attention span of the audience, who started to titter and fidget while Beatrice hissed instructions to get the music back on track.

At this moment, the door suddenly crashed open, and a characteristic clattering and clinking heralded the arrival of the tea trolley. The residents noisily indicated their approval of this diversion. With relief and embarrassment in equal measure, the players gave up the unequal fight and withdrew gracefully.

"Well, we were never going to play that at the wedding anyway," Donald blustered defensively, as the players took their tea in an anteroom.

"That's not the point," Beatrice fumed, slamming her cup down. "You really must concentrate harder, you mustn't let yourself get confused under stress, I'm the leader, it's my reputation on the line if it goes wrong, I can't afford..."

"Don't be too hard on him," Charles interrupted. "He didn't *have* to do this playing today. And his sound does blend very well with ours. It's *my* wedding gig, remember, and I'm sure it'll all go fine."

Charles met the bride at the function room for the usual music-planning meeting, and marvelled at the new generation of brides – they all had a clear idea in their minds of their whole ceremony, in detail, from start to finish. Indeed, he couldn't remember ever having a planning meeting where any parent or bridegroom was to be seen. He occasionally wondered whether the amount spent on the wedding was inversely related to the length of the subsequent marriage, but kept his thoughts to himself.

After discussing the general type of music she would like played while the guests were assembling, the bride asked, "Can I come in to the famous Wedding March, like I would in church?"

"Yes, I know the one you mean, we can play it, but it doesn't sound quite the same with a string trio as with a full church organ, not in a reception room like this, with all these carpets and curtains and drapes soaking up the sound. And, I don't know what the local Registrar's attitude is, but I was told off for playing it once..."

"Told off?"

"Yes! Your music must have no religious connotations whatever – that's a rule for registry weddings. This particular registrar, he said, didn't I know that the Wagner Wedding March was for Lohengrin's wedding in the opera, and Lohengrin was a Knight of the Holy Grail, and that made it religious. But don't worry, if *you* want it, I'll play it."

"Well, what else can I have? Not a silly military march, please."

"OK, there's a conventional one, and..," Charles pondered for a moment whether he should suggest it, "...an off-the-wall one."

"Yes, I like off-the-wall. If it can't be conventional, well, I'll have off-the-wall. What is it?"

Charles regretted his impulse, but was forced to go on with it. The bride laughed at his efforts to hum the tune.

"Can you please walk, at the speed, you'll be doing on the day, from the entrance door to the registrar's table, while I time you?"

Charles set the stopwatch on his phone and hummed the piece in his head while she test-walked, and when she arrived at where the groom would be standing, he subtracted the time from the length of the piece.

"That's good," he said, "On the day, get your bridesmaid to signal you've arrived, then we'll start playing. Get her to count off 1 minute, then come in through the door exactly like you just did."

"A *minute*? It won't take even *me* that long to sort my dress and then come in looking duly radiant. You must have something better?"

Charles was secretly relieved. What a risky choice it would have been, all the ways it could have gone wrong...

"I was asking you..." said the bride.

"Yes, sorry," Charles collected himself, "I was just thinking. For your big day, perhaps conventional is best after all – something that will sound right to your guests. Hm, the Entrance of the Queen of Sheba is familiar and very effective, but, no, too long for what you're wanting. Well,

58

there's always Pachelbel's Canon. The big advantage of the Pachelbel is that it has, well, sort-of landing-places, every ten seconds or so, where we can stop and it feels like a proper ending."

"So I can walk in, get to the registrar's table, and the music stops within ten seconds, guaranteed? Yes I'll have it!"

"Just one thing. The piece takes a while to get going, and it'd sound odd, incomplete, if we had to stop *too* soon. It starts with some long notes. I know you won't want to hang around once you've arrived, you've just told me, but *please* count off sixteen long notes, more if you like, before you enter."

On the day, when Donald and Beatrice arrived to join Charles, they were surprised at how tight was the corner in which they were expected to play.

"I can see why you told us only a trio would fit in here. How come you got this gig anyway?"

"Well, the previous time, I was a very-last-minute stand-in when the leader's normal viola couldn't do it. The leader's on the 'recommended-suppliers' list that this venue hands out when you book here – and he got them to add me, I suppose in gratitude that I'd saved the day for him. Anyway, that's enough chit-chat, we have work to do, because, yes, I think I saw possibly some wedding guests already in the lounge. So, let's get ourselves set up now and start playing our selections, and then they should start coming in."

They started with a movement of the K563, on the basis that the rest of their playlist would then seem easy. A few guests wandered in and seemed to enjoy it.

As the trio continued playing their selections, the room filled up and the groom and registrar took up their places. Soon, Charles noticed the bride's entrance door open slightly and a little girl's hand waved through it.

"OK, we've got the signal, she's here. Stop this number at the next double bar," hissed Charles. He was not of course the leader, but as it was his gig, he was in charge. "Donald, start the Pachelbel now please, nice and steady. What d'you mean, you don't have the part? For goodness sake, of course you don't have a part. Clot! Can't you remember anything? We practised it, - you have the same sequence of eight crotchets in D major, twenty-eight times... oh merciful heavens, you remember now."

As Beatrice and Charles both counted off the first eight crotchets, they were surprised to see the bride push through the door past a bridesmaid trying to restrain her. Charles could hardly believe this was the same composed young lady with whom he'd had the music planning meeting. She hadn't counted off 16, not even 8, when she broke free from her bridesmaid, raced towards the registrar's table, knocked over a flower display in her haste, rushed up to the groom and smothered him in enthusiastic kisses. Clearly, having got her man to this point, she wasn't going to waste a further moment.

As the registrar started the proceedings, Charles recollected his previous wedding job here. That bride had insisted on entering to the slow movement of Beethoven's string trio Opus 3, a most unusual choice. For her, it had worked brilliantly. The music had an inbuilt rising sense of expectation leading to her entrance, which she had timed so accurately that she reached the registrar's table at the exact moment the trio reached the end of the exposition. It was a triumph.

But what a disaster if Charles had succeeded in foisting this piece on *today's* bride!

When the registrar ended with his customary "You may kiss the bride", there was nervous laughter before the guests applauded and took pictures on their phones and cameras. After the couple had posed and smiled, the bride nodded to Charles, who signalled to start the adaptation for string trio of Mendelssohn's Wedding March As the couple marched out to this traditional piece, a welcome and almost palpable air of normality was restored.

When the guests had left, a waitress entered, as pre-arranged, with tea and sandwiches for the musicians. As they put aside the cleaning and packing of their instruments, they noticed two gentlemen returning who had been among the first to sit down when the music originally started – it seemed hours ago.

"I'm sorry to interrupt your well-earned refreshment," the first gentleman addressed them, "but let me introduce myself. I'm the parish priest of the groom, and it grieves me that he chose to be married here, but that's by-the-by.

My church is used extensively for community activities, and I'm asking - indeed, taking the unwarranted liberty of asking - whether you would consider playing in it, to benefit the new lighting fund."

Donald, anxious to shake off the reputation he felt he was probably acquiring as a hopeless liability to the trio, surprised them by immediately answering, "Yes, I'm up for it."

So Beatrice and Charles were forced to agree.

The second gentleman spoke. "Well, as you've shown yourselves so community-minded, here's your reward. I'm rebuilding that restaurant on the bypass..."

"Oh, yes, I know the one. Near the country park. All closed off, covered in scaffolding and dust-sheets."

"Yes, that's the one. Well, I want you to play at the grand re-opening. Now, as you're doing the Reverend here a favour for free, it's only fair I'll pay you full professional rates, and, *of course,* a meal."

Both events went well, greatly helped by the uncannily matching tone of the three instruments. Donald wondered how long he would be allowed to stay in Beatrice and Charles's trio. He felt a fraud next to them – his technique was so superficial and hit-and-miss while theirs was so solid and reliable. And he kept making silly mistakes, such as playing in the wrong key, or playing repeats where they'd agreed not to, or counting rests wrongly - although the latter was becoming less of an issue as he became more familiar with their functions-and-events repertoire.

    Some time later, Beatrice called the other two together at a Chiltern Phil rehearsal.
"I was at the weekly lunchtime concert in the town centre where I work, well, I go often enough for the organiser to recognise me as a regular. So I wasn't surprised when he asked if I knew any groups that would like to perform – travelling expenses only, no fee I'm afraid... Well, yes, we could play our usual repertoire, but they have a fabulous piano there in the church, kept in tip-top condition, and I've had this ambition, for years, to play Schubert's piano trio Opus 99. Charles, do I remember you telling me you were originally a student of violin *and piano*?"

This concert took a great deal of organising, as Charles and Donald had no hope of fitting the concert (including travelling) into their respective working days and would both have to take a day's leave. Rehearsals were no easier, as there was some argument about which one of the three of them had the most suitable piano at home, and, all being in regular employment, their leisure-time diaries were crammed.

Once they had rehearsed at Charles's and had sampled his wife's coffee and home-made cakes, there was no further dispute about where to rehearse.

As the rehearsals of the Op99 progressed, Charles and Donald could see why Beatrice had wanted to perform it. Donald was becoming quite a fan of the slow movement, and though he was interpreting it quite well, Beatrice would always be picking him up on technical points, until, one day:

"Look, Donald," said Beatrice, "this slow movement is so sublime, it's Schubert baring his innermost feelings, it's seeing into his very soul. It does **not** need a heavy beat at the barline at the end of the every phrase like you're giving it. Yes, I know it's something that cellists, bass players too, just habitually do, give a strong beat on barlines at ends of phrases, it's probably what you got taught but just pay attention, listen to where the harmony and the phrasing are going, for goodness sake use your musical sensitivity. This music is much gentler, the phrases just want to flow together, sometimes the end of the phrase doesn't want a thumpy beat, sometimes it wants no stress at all. Sometimes, even, it wants to fade away, yes even at the beginning of a bar."

Donald was used to Beatrice's normal comments, but stunned by this one. It was so earnestly heart-felt on her part, while so challenging to his lifelong notion that he was there mainly to provide the sense of rhythm and harmonic floor to the ensemble.

Before their next rehearsal meeting, he practised ending all phrases on a diminuendo, so that he would be used to doing it wherever required, even when it seemed to make no sense in the particular passages he was playing. It was highly counter-intuitive to him, but he began to be able to do it without feeling too self-conscious or pretentious.

"Donald!" exclaimed Beatrice at their next rehearsal, "Your phrasing-off - you're beginning to understand - you really were listening to what I said! What do you think of the music now?"

"Well, the music has an extra dimension..."

"Yes? how?"

"Er, it has colours and tints."

"While before..?"

"Oh, it had shape and beauty and meaning, but it's, ah, three-dimensional now."

"My word, Donald, I knew you must be clever to be an actuary, but, well, you might even have the makings of a musician."

Charles plinked a chord on the piano to remind them he was there. "Do I detect romance in the air?"

"Absolutely not!" Beatrice thundered, "How dare you!" Calming a little, she continued, "Not since, not since, hm, it was at music college... Well, in short, I don't think I can ever trust a man again."

"Oh dear, sorry, I didn't mean to touch a nerve," said Charles, "and now I've put my foot in it, this is the worst time to ask you a difficult question that's on my mind."

"All right, ask away."

"Beatrice, please don't take this the wrong way because I know this concert is your project, and I know you really really want to do the Schubert, but, this slow movement, it's so good, and... I must admit I'm not finding the other movements all that easy. If it were left to me, I'd sooner do just this movement of the Schubert, maybe as the centre-piece of the concert. It's only 40 minutes they want isn't it? So we could do lighter, salon-type stuff before and after."

After a long tense pause, Beatrice said slowly, "Do you know, you might be right. Now we've been working properly on the Schubert, I'm beginning to think, yes, you might have a point - the slow movement *is* better than the others. So," she continued, more decisively now, "if we don't play the other movements, nobody will be comparing. Yes, salon-type will go down well at lunchtime. How about you, Donald?"

"Yes, fine by me." He was pleased, as he was finding he was having to gear-change his style between the Schubert movements, but had been reluctant to say so for fear of appearing precious.

Beatrice found some light piano-trio arrangements of folk tunes and popular Italian arias, and a couple of Frank Bridge piano-trio miniatures, which she could lead without stress and which were effective without being too technically demanding for the piano or cello.

On the day, the three assembled mid-morning at the church, only to find it locked. Charles wandered round to see if there was a side door, which, in this high-street location, there wasn't. Meanwhile, Beatrice got on her mobile to each likely number on the outside noticeboard but was diverted to voicemail each time.

A lady passing by stopped and asked, "What, are you today's concert? And hasn't anyone let you in? That's disgraceful, don't know what's gone wrong. Ha, look, they're expecting you, that's you three on this concert poster isn't it? Hm, I know the churchwarden's wife - she works in that shop over there, I'll have a word," at which she trotted off.

In a moment, she returned with a gigantic key that looked more like a museum relic than the real thing, but it released the door, and in a few minutes, with the aid of the lady, the lights and heating were switched on.

As the trio set up, more helpers came in, summoned by Beatrice's voicemails and by the churchwarden via his wife. One of the helpers brought a box of biscuits, put on a kettle, and offered the trio refreshments.

After such a confused start, the actual task of rehearsing seemed simple. Charles was glad to find the piano every bit as good as Beatrice had promised. A small group of overseas tourists wandered in, and Beatrice took the opportunity of standing up and practising her announcement of the next item. This had the unintended effect that the tourists got up with every sign of embarrassment and shuffled out, under the misapprehension that they'd been ordered out.

A quarter-hour before the advertised start, the trio put down their instruments and sat to one side. The organiser came up to Beatrice to apologise for the earlier disorganisation and to check how the trio wanted to be introduced.

The refreshment helper soon ran out of supplies as unexpected numbers entered the church. The other helpers were bemused but were able to shoe-horn everyone in.

All went well, and then the Schubert. Beatrice said a few words about her long-standing ambition to play this, and after a few moments for all three to get in the mood, Beatrice nodded.

The ensemble was perfect. The musical mood carried everyone with it. The harmonies cried to heaven. How could a mere human have composed this perfection? The music was of unbearable beauty, all the players instinctively co-ordinating their phrasing, even their breathing. As the sound spilled into the street outside, some passers-by came in and stood in wonderment at the back. The players were all sharing the same extraordinary, even transcendental, insight into the meaning of the piece and their part in it.

At the end, there was a long silence, before a steady appreciative applause. Beatrice stood up to speak but was lost for words. She was regretting now that this wasn't the last item in the programme, but would be followed by a couple of much shallower pieces.

Eventually she muttered something to the audience about the remaining pieces not being at this emotional level, and the trio did their best with the arrangements of sentimental Italian arias and folk ditties.

At the end, the players started to focus on the audience – when entering, it was normal for players to pretend to be looking at the audience while actually fixing their eyes on a chandelier or an Exit sign, to avoid distraction by any individual. Now free to pay attention to the individuals making up the audience, Beatrice was amazed when she saw her boss walking up.

"A lot of our clients came to see you. I spoke to some of them, and they were thrilled, even those who thought chamber music was boring, and only came out of loyalty or curiosity."

Then Donald in turn was amazed to see one of the top partners of his actuarial firm come up to speak. All the way from the office in central London! Finally it was Charles's turn, as his wife, as well as the manager of his A&E department, joined the group of admirers.

The organiser came up beaming. "This is by far our biggest collection. We can make a start on restoring the stonework. Can you come again?"

They shook their heads in exhaustion. Donald managed to say "No, couldn't repeat it. Something happened just then. I'm not spiritual, but something just... happened."

At length, the trio, with Beatrice's boss, moved out into the street and fell into a coffee shop. As the lunch hour was just over, they easily found a comfortable window table, and could at last tuck in. Just like sportsmen, and for the same reasons, musicians avoided eating directly before appearing in public.

"So how do we follow that?" asked Charles.

They stopped talking as a very superior lady in very superior hat, coat and gloves walked slowly past and looked into the window. She about-turned and in a few moments she appeared inside the coffee shop standing at their table.

"What a stroke of luck!" she said, "All of you together. And you," indicating the optician, "you must be their agent."

"No," spluttered Beatrice's boss, "I'm your optician. I'm privileged to have Beatrice here as a valued colleague in my practice."

"Oh, silly me, fancy me not recognising you, it must be some problem with my specs, oops, what a silly thing to say, anyway, I'm glad I've caught you all, because in my circle of friends we occasionally have music parties at each others' houses, perhaps two different ensembles, thirty or forty minutes from each, you're paid of course, then a buffet supper. We like speaking to musicians, because we can immediately grasp their fantastic talent, and it fascinates us, as we ourselves don't have an ounce of musical ability between us, though we really do love it."

"Were you hoping for the Schubert...?" Beatrice started, when the superior lady interrupted: "Oh no, I don't have a piano, I was thinking of string trio music – I remember you three from the grand re-opening of that restaurant on the bypass. Oh, and I was there when you did the same piece for helping that church, very noble of you."

A date was decided for the soirée, everyone exchanged contact details and the lady departed.

"Is this what the music world is?" asked Beatrice's boss, "All glamorous invitations to posh houses through chance meetings? I'm in the wrong business."

As they tucked into their well-earned toasted savouries and coffee, Charles mused, "Well, her audience is probably fairly clued-up about music – we could be quite serious – some movements from K563, now we know she's already heard it? The piece seems to suit us."

"True," said Donald, becoming bolder and willing to put a musical point of view within the trio, "It is called 'Divertimento' after all, music for diversion. She doesn't want an hour's playing from us, which is practically what it would take. I'm sure Mozart would have expected just a few movements to be played if that's what the patron wanted."

So, at their next rehearsal, they decided to include the first movement, with its attention-grabbing (if done well) slow downward arpeggio leading to an extraordinary development of such a simple start.

Despite the contretemps at the old-folks' home, Donald wanted to do the next movement, the Adagio, and this too was agreed.

"So how long are those two movements?" he asked Beatrice.

"Eleven minutes plus 9½ minutes, so, just over 20."

"Is that with or without repeats?" persisted Donald in a slightly cheeky tone.

"It's doing the first repeat and not the second in each case, which would be the usual thing. See, I've marked all that on my part, the first repeat of the first movement is 3 minutes 10 seconds and then..."

"Yes, fine, all right," said Donald, who made a mental note not to try to wrong-foot Beatrice again, and fell silent.

They all wanted to include the last movement, an Allegro conveying a happy carefree "end-of-term" feeling. This left an Andante theme-and-variations, which never went well in rehearsal, and two Minuet&Trio movements; it was then fairly easy to agree to omit the Andante and one of the minuets.

They would thus be playing four of the six movements, which, according to Beatrice, would add up to 35 minutes, just as the lady wanted.

To avoid parking problems, the three agreed to meet at Charles's and to go together in his large family car to the lady's house.

As they followed the satnav, they were taken along lanes they had never seen before, and then up an obscure winding drive, ending at a fine mansion completely hidden from the road. The gravelled area in front of the entrance was well populated with fine high-prestige cars.

"My, there's money in this county," marvelled Beatrice.

"There's so much parking area here, we could easily have driven separately," said Donald, "except our old bangers would have lowered the tone – oh look, *there* are musicians, look at those two rust-buckets parked just over there."

"*Aaargh! That's Araminta's car! Over there!*" squeaked Beatrice.

"Who's Araminta?" asked Donald innocently.

Charles explained, "Araminta leads nearly everything round here. She leads the Downs Ensemble, the best chamber orchestra in these parts. She's always popping up in orchestra pits for the operatic societies – usually leading. When she's not doing sessions for one or other of the London orchestras, she's often brought in by local amateur orchestra to stiffen the first violins. She really has the presence, the aura, the charisma, of a Leader. She can stop a brass section in full flight with a single raised eyebrow."

Realising, too late, that this explanation to Donald was not calculated to reassure Beatrice, he added, "But Beatrice, you'll be absolutely fine, we're with you all the way. All that rehearsal, it'll pay off now. No need to worry, really there isn't."

The three of them unloaded their instrument cases and walked to the door.

"Just let me take a few deep breaths before we ring the bell," said Beatrice, "...Thank you, that's better, I feel OK now."

As they were being ushered into the musicians' green room, Beatrice froze.

"It's him, it's the man from music college!!"

"All right," said Charles, "I'll keep him away from you."

There was no need, as the man in question looked equally shocked when he recognised Beatrice. His body language made it clear that he would definitely avoid her.

Beatrice approached Araminta timidly. "Nice to see you. Are you on first? String quartets?"

"Ah, it's Beatrice, isn't it?" responded Araminta graciously, "section principal in the Chiltern Phil and with a superb violin? Yes, I remember you, we've played together in concerts and pits. Anyway, I think your group is on first. Good luck. You'll get on famously; they're a most appreciative bunch of friends she has."

Araminta's cellist then arrived. She looked slightly familiar, but Beatrice couldn't place her.

More concerning to Beatrice was that Araminta was behaving as if her group was now complete – not a quartet, but another string *trio*. Head-to-head comparison. Could it get any worse than this?

Charles and Donald were quite insensitive to all this, and set up and tuned as if it were a casual rehearsal. Beatrice then joined them, sensing she would get no particular emotional support from them but relieved on the other hand that they seemed quite free of sense-of-occasion nerves.

At length, the hostess asked the guests to take their seats, and announced the players.

Beatrice then stood and spoke briefly about the Mozart piece they were about to perform, much as Charles had done so long ago at the old folks' home. She added a feeble joke about how far-sighted Mozart was to write a piece for this combination, violin+viola+cello: If a group was assembling to play string quartets, it was fifty-fifty that the last to arrive would be a violinist, so, while waiting, the three who had been punctual could start playing this trio. There were some chuckles from the audience. Beatrice sat down, the three looked at each other, and smiled.

A preparatory glance and nod from Beatrice, and the opening E-flat arpeggio sounded in perfect ensemble and unison. This was a good start. The hours of rehearsal had indeed paid off, as Charles had predicted. The room acoustics were just right. Even Donald was paying intense attention. He slightly fluffed a notoriously awkward showpiece passage a few moments before the end of the first movement, but he kept in time, and it was the sort of minor incident that made live music more exciting and real than any recording.

Donald excelled himself in the following slow movement, his favourite. The cello sets the mood and tempo, and he gave a clear steady lead.

Soon, the three were playing for themselves, concentrating only on each other and, almost before they knew it, they were embarking on the joyous 'end-of-term' final movement. Although they knew it well, they had never been able to make sense of a particular disruptive rhythmic figure which intrudes out of nowhere to form maybe a bridging passage or maybe a second subject. This time, telepathically, they treated it as a foretaste (albeit syncopated) of the closing flourish. In this vein, they tossed it to each other, revelling in its various articulations, until its final appearance as the triumphant coda of the piece.

The audience responded with warmly appreciative applause. The hostess said some complimentary words and invited her guests to recharge their glasses while Araminta's group set themselves up for the second half. Out of the corner of her eye, Beatrice saw anxious conversation going on within Araminta's camp, which was completely ignored by Donald and Charles, who were concentrating on the drinks and nibbles.

Donald muttered to Charles, "That joke by Beatrice, I think she got her sums wrong. The odds *aren't* 50:50. Mozart would have usually played viola, so the three people coming round to his place to play string quartets would surely have been two violins and a cello, so the odds that they could play his trio while waiting for the last one to arrive, would be *two-thirds*."

"Oh, Donald, really," replied Charles between mouthfuls, "only an actuary would come up with that!"

The hostess called for everyone to return to their seats, and gestured for Araminta to speak.

"It's an honour to be here with you again," she started. "I had expected to bring you a string quartet as I usually do, but, well, I won't bore you with why, this time it's a string trio, same as you've just heard so superbly led by Beatrice. Now, there's not a huge amount of trio repertoire, compared with string quartets. So, you've maybe guessed what I'm going to say - we were planning to play some of the exact same movements as you've just heard! But you didn't hear the *fourth* movement of the Mozart trio, so we'll start with that, then some Pleyel, finishing with some Boccherini."

"We'll hear some virtuoso stuff from all three of them," whispered Donald. "Pleyel wrote…"

"*Shush.*"

The fourth movement of the Mozart started, as Beatrice's trio knew well, with a statement of a theme akin to an artless folk melody. As the variations unfolded, they displayed a relentless logic and structure which had always eluded Beatrice's trio. Charles dropped his head into his hands. Not only had he always failed his leader in this movement, he was being shown up by another viola player, and not just any viola player, but one who had obviously wronged Beatrice in some serious way.

Beatrice was nearly in tears at the commanding performance of this movement, so superior to anything which she had managed. Eventually, at the B-flat-minor section of the movement, even Donald could see that Araminta's trio was outclassing them, and slumped down in his seat in despair.

Araminta then took the demisemiquavers of the final Maggiore section at such a breakneck tempo that Donald secretly hoped that her viola and cello would stumble when it was their turn to play them. His unworthy thoughts were trumped by impeccably accurate and unhurried renditions from, first the viola, and then the cello.

At the end of the movement, Beatrice, Donald and Charles were all too shattered by the brilliance they had heard, to join in the applause.

The promised trios by Pleyel and Boccherini were then performed, with good ensemble and with the solo passages for each instrument capably and confidently played. During the strong applause at the end, Charles whispered, "Hey, they weren't expecting to play those this evening, but they were so on-top of them, they must have used them as warm-up pieces in their practice sessions." The other two nodded.

The hostess said a few words of thanks, and continued, "Now, as always, I would really like you all to stay for refreshments. But let the musicians get to the table first!"

She led the way to a generous buffet laid out in a nearby room. Beatrice realised with dread that she would have to make small talk with Araminta's group, but Charles second-guessed her and button-holed Araminta.

"I did so admire your viola player's technique," said Charles, almost choking on his words, "I don't see him, I was hoping to have a word with him maybe?"

"Oh, he said he'd had a text and would have to go home at once. Some domestic emergency, I didn't quite gather. Very unlike him to pass up on a buffet like this. But I'll be sure to pass on your compliments."

Charles looked round, caught Beatrice's eye, and silently mouthed to her "He's gone home."

Beatrice relaxed visibly and went up to Araminta. Soon, plates of canapés in hand, they were deep in conversation about shoulder rests and makes of rosin.

"About those split notes that made you change your violin," asked Araminta, "do you use fabric softener when you wash your violin duster? Well, that might be what caused it, traces of fabric conditioner transferred to the string and making your bow skid. Nothing to do with your violin, but it doesn't matter, you certainly did right to get such a good one."

Charles coughed, to remind the violinists that they were meant to mingle with the guests. The musicians then circulated among the company, conversing politely. Charles was relieved to see even Donald falling into line on this.

As the guests started to leave, the hostess came up to the musicians, speaking to them individually and thanking them all warmly. She then returned to her remaining guests, her closer friends. The five musicians came together and stood for a few moments. Araminta broke the silence.

"Beatrice, would your trio like to join me to form a string quartet?"

"*You* want to lead *us*?" exclaimed Beatrice, dumbfounded. "Why?"

"The last movement of your K563. Your interpretation answered a lot of the questions that have bothered me about it."

"What about your cellist?" asked Donald in a rare moment of sensitivity, "won't *she* want to...?"

"Oh, that's all right – but really, I should let Zoë speak for herself..."

"Oh, you're *Zoë*," interrupted Charles, "I thought I recognised you but I just couldn't place you, it's seeing you drive a cello and not your usual double bass. Downs Ensemble. Of course."

"Yes," said Zoë, "and that's exactly why I'm not looking for string quartet playing right now – I've got too much bass work on. So, you three, please go right ahead and join up with Araminta if you want, that really is absolutely fine by me."

"But you're such an ace cellist," said Donald, wonderingly, "Your solo bits up in the snow in the Pleyel..."

"You're too kind," she said dismissively, "and it's been great talking to you, but I really must be off home now - early start tomorrow." With that, she packed her instrument and bits and pieces, and left.

The four got out their phones (or, in Charles's case, a paper diary) to make a date. With their respective busy lives, the soonest date they could find for this new string quartet to have its first meeting was two months ahead.

"What if something comes up, shouldn't we have a reserve date?"

"No," said Araminta, "the London orchestras that book me last-minute will be in recess..."

"Well," persisted Charles, "it could be anything, for any of us – jury service, say."

"All right."

So they made a second date even further ahead.

"What are you planning to play?" asked Beatrice, anxious for her three to practise thoroughly in advance, so as to not to upset Araminta's rather misplaced faith (as Beatrice saw it) in their abilities.

"Oh, let's not worry about that now," said Araminta airily, with the confidence of one well grounded in the repertoire, "Let's decide when we meet. I've plenty of music to choose from."

"That's exactly what I was afraid of," said Beatrice as soon as Araminta was out of hearing. "What'll she throw at us?"

"The Ravel?" suggested Donald gloomily, "Starts impossible then gets harder."

"A late Shostakovitch? A late Beethoven even? Or Bax or Walton?" threw in Charles.

"Well, let's just all practise our sight-reading," proposed Beatrice. "Sit in for the concerts of any orchestra you can find – we're all Chilterns Phil, they should welcome us, well, maybe."

6. Quartet

When the day came, they gathered nervously at Araminta's house, sat down even more nervously, and tuned more nervously still.

"How about a little Mozart to warm up?" said Araminta, in a tone that indicated this was a decision not a question. "You play Mozart well."

Just as the others were breathing more easily, Araminta handed out parts. "I think, one of the *King of Prussia* quartets."

The King in question, who had commissioned the set of three quartets now named after him, was a capable cellist, and Mozart had obliged with duly showy cello parts, written actually with the virtuoso cellist Duport in mind.

Donald put on a brave face, and Araminta signalled to start. Not an expansive signal, quite restrained in fact, but somehow her speed and rhythmic intentions transmitted themselves to her players with the clarity of whipcracks. I don't know how she does it, thought Donald, but no wonder she's so successful and in such demand as a leader.

Early on in the piece, slightly uncertain as to a viola entry, Charles sensed a pulse radiating from Araminta, onto which he could latch, and entered spot-on. I don't know how she does it, thought Charles, but no wonder she's so successful and in such demand as a leader.

As Donald reached his first showpiece passage in the first movement, he misjudged a position shift and had to adjust his pitch, he thought quite unobtrusively. Araminta stopped (at which, everyone else did, instantly) and looked at Donald expressionlessly and silently. What psychology, thought Beatrice; Araminta has worked out, from hardly knowing him, that Donald needs taking down a peg, she's let him see his weakness, and he's learned his lesson, all without her saying anything; I don't know how she does it, but no wonder she's so successful and in such demand as a leader.

Donald moved his efforts up a gear, playing less ostentatiously, but more accurately and more as one of the team. They reached the end of the quartet.

"Yes," said Araminta, "I hoped it would be like this. I think we can play together... there's something else odd, our tones blend so well, I can't fathom it. Let's have an early coffee."

Over coffee and biscuits, she started to tell the story of how she found her violin:

"That goes back to when I was teaching violin for a couple of the London Boroughs."

"A *couple*? How did you juggle them?"

"Oh, no!" she laughed, "I didn't have to juggle!" The others had never heard her laugh before. Maybe, despite her musical perfection, she was human after all.

She continued, "You see, the two Boroughs shared their music staff, we worked half-time in each. Then I got on the 'extras' list of the London Opera. Did wonders for my sight-reading. Oh...", she stopped herself, recalling the question she'd been asked, "still no juggling, it fitted in well with the school day. Well actually, still on the juggling metaphor, I did drop a ball – I was getting so much opera work, my husband couldn't take it and left me."

"Oh," said Charles, "oh dear, I *am* sorry."

"Hazard of the music profession I'm afraid. Musical marriages often fail – the unsocial hours, or one of you is more successful than the other. That can be hard to take. Or you're *both* successful and then you can't plan ahead to spend time together – a gig will come up just when you don't want, but you don't dare turn anything down. And you can't even be sure to have meals together – they'll suddenly call a rehearsal for some silly time that suits *them*, like noon or 4pm. It's all against any normal married domestic existence."

Beatrice and Charles began to appreciate the pressures that had shaped Araminta's character.

"But you haven't said about your violin," butted in Donald with his leaden-footed tactlessness.

"Ah, yes, what happened was, my desk partner in the opera pit said something about my violin not projecting, which I thought was a cheek as you can only judge that from the auditorium. What? Cheek? No, of course I didn't say *that* to *him*, I was an extra on a zero-hours contract. But I did ask the conductor, who did eventually say I would probably get more work in the firsts if I had a stronger violin."

As Donald made to interrupt again, Araminta returned to her usual impersonal self, announcing, "That's enough chit-chat for now. We need to play another quartet, get used to each other, build a sense of ensemble. How about..., how about, the Ravel?"

Donald remembered how he had already been silently rebuked by Araminta, and realised he had now brought the Ravel on himself. He supposed he deserved it, but began to see that his behaviour was also punishing Beatrice and Charles, who wouldn't find the Ravel simple either.

So they started to tackle the Ravel and were beginning to make reasonable fist of the first movement – the easiest – when....

"Stop!" shouted Beatrice in exasperation, "I'm piggy-in-the-middle here. There's you Donald, playing metronomically, and there's you Araminta, playing artistically. And Charles, you, you're about as much use as a, as a..."

"As a viola?" he suggested helpfully.

"Please, please, everybody, take a breath," said Araminta. "Thank you. You see, there's a balance. In music there's always a balance. Well, not one specific balance, more a *range* of acceptable balances. The music doesn't want to be so artistic that it collapses into jelly, but then it doesn't want to be so machine-rhythmic, so like a synthesiser, that it loses all feeling. Think of it this way - With one ear, you listen to your own playing, check it's in tune, in time, right dynamic. Your other ear, you listen to everybody else – compared with them, are you drifting one way or the other, or too loud, too soft, too legato, too detached – fit in, be ready to adjust, moment by moment. If you can, look up from your parts, look round, see the gestures, see the body language of the others. If the inner parts ever complain about being piggy-in-the-middle, that's a failing of the whole quartet," she concluded diplomatically, looking however pointedly at Donald.

The first movement was tackled reasonably but Ravel's difficulties of ensemble and rhythm now began to escalate.

After an uncomfortable further hour on the Ravel, Araminta said, "That wasn't easy, it wasn't meant to be. But yes, you three do work, you do listen, you are prepared to take my leadership.

Right, get out your diaries, this is going to be a regular quartet."

In subsequent sessions, the story of her violin came out, how her quest had taken her to dealers and auction houses, how she had found nothing that was exactly right for her.

She had then been picked to join the London Opera's touring production for the next summer's Edinburgh Festival, and seized her chance to try Edinburgh's violin shops.

"So this particular dealer let me try a few – he seemed to be assessing my playing style and looking out what he though would suit me. I moved to his next violin and was struck how dull it looked. But its tone was so unexpected – not its volume, but something about the clarity of its projection. I took it on approval and tried it in the pit that evening. The conductor even beamed at me. So that decided me."

As she went into her kitchen to make coffee, she went back in her mind to that time...

Back then, the morning after her decision, Araminta skipped the opera company's private sight-seeing tour, to return to the dealer. He was quite happy to tell her the history of the violin.

"It was brought here," he said, "for me to sell on commission. The owner's completely given up playing now, but when he came to retire a few years back, he was full-time second-desk on the firsts of the Caledonian Orchestra, oh yes, a fine player... but he'd hoped to rise further in his career. That's why he bought the violin in the first place. He'd been appointed to the Caledonian, this was back in the 1970s, he had Leadership ambitions and he wanted a credible violin. He was lucky - just as he started looking, this violin came into Edinburgh's main auction house. It had been put in for quick sale by a firm of bankruptcy practitioners..."

"...who had no idea what it was," suggested Araminta.

"Well, they half-did," explained the dealer. "The family that owned it had gone bust in the Scottish oil boom..."

"Went bust? in your oil boom?"

"Yes, by borrowing money to speculate in land. You see, they were crofters in the Shetlands, overpaying to buy any bit of land that they thought might be needed for new oil terminals. Well, that was their big idea, but the Zetland Council was worried about what all this oil development would do to the natural environment, and so it forced all the oil companies to share the one existing terminal. So the family were left with all this unsaleable land and couldn't pay their debts."

"But the violin?" asked Araminta.

"Oh, yes, the family included some fine folk-fiddlers, going back generations, who'd been playing reels on this violin at ceilidhs all round the Shetlands. The bankruptcy practitioners realised it must be a good violin and would fetch a better price at auction down here in Edinburgh."

"And that's when the Caledonian Orchestra man bought it? My word, what a fascinating tale."

"Oh, but there's more," said the dealer, with the air of a magician about to pull a rabbit out of a hat, "It's amazing really. Someone in the auction house had this hunch and went through their archives. And, sure enough, they found the sale particulars of this selfsame violin, way back in 1815."

"So, back then, it would have been only a few years old, hardly played in."

"Yes, just so. The vendor's name didn't mean anything to the auction house, but the winning bidder's name did – it was Lord Shetland. The auction-house ledger has a note that it was for his fiddler. It passed down the fiddler's family, and, by all these twists and turns, into your hands. So now you know."

Araminta returned with coffee and biscuits, and summarised the story of her violin going back just to the crofters' bankruptcy. Its earlier story, she thought, was so impossibly romantic that it would only bore her quartet, besides which, there was still that tantalising gap about its first few years.

Eventually Charles broke the silence. "Shetlands, eh, Shetlands?" He went strangely quiet and his eyes seemed to go misty. Collecting himself, he continued, "Yes, well, after all that, d'you know who made it?"

"Here," said Araminta with rare openness as she handed him her violin, "see for yourself."

As his eyes adjusted and focussed on the label inside, he gasped, "I'm seeing things, I don't believe it, *'Matthew Hardie, Edinburgh, 1811'.*"

"So what don't you believe?"

"All right, look at my viola. Then look at Beatrice's violin. No, Donald's cello isn't interesting."

"Well then," announced Araminta, "we must call ourselves the Hardie Quartet. Donald, you don't mind, I hope?"

"No, fine by me. Reflected glory and all that."

The Hardie Quartet's audiences were initially attracted to its concerts and recitals on the strength of Araminta being the Leader, but in time the Quartet achieved corporate recognition in its own right.

One day, Charles came to rehearsal seeming distracted.

"What's the trouble, Charles?"

"Oh, sorry, no, there's no trouble. It's nothing really. You know it's my turn this month to receive the <info@hardiequartet> emails; well, one's just come in from a Katrina Young.

She says she's making a study of Scottish violin makers, and wants to meet us."

"So, that's good, isn't it? Anything that raises our profile…"

"Yes of course. I'm just being silly. Years ago there was a Katrina – even now, I can't see the name without reacting – but it's silly. I checked the name out on the internet and the nearest hit I got was a string teacher in Florida. So it's not *that* Katrina, don't know why I'm making such a fuss."

Solid dependable Charles, well well well.

At their next meeting, Araminta made an announcement.

"Zoë's been in touch, you remember, my cellist at that soirée where we all first met. Beatrice, did you say you played piano?"

"Yes, and I have some private pupils, but if Zoë wants a pianist, Charles plays much better, we did a Schubert piano trio…"

"No Beatrice, it has to be you. Charles won't do, too long since he's played violin, and I haven't played viola in ages. But I'm really glad you said Schubert."

"Oh, please Araminta," said Charles, "I had a rough time in my A&E shift last night, my brain can't take all these puzzles, what *are* you talking about?"

"It's perfectly simple," explained Araminta severely, "Zoë wants to play The Trout with us. Fundraising concert for a charity of hers. Easy, it all falls into place if Beatrice will swap to piano. Ah, Donald, you're all right, you're still our cello for this; Zoë will play double bass."

7. Trout

The first date suitable for all five to meet for rehearsal was several weeks ahead. While the four string players gave the impression that they would have met tomorrow if their diaries had permitted it, Beatrice was secretly pleased at the extra time she had, to refamiliarise herself with the piano part.

When the day came, Beatrice prepared her music room, laid out ready for this ensemble.

Zoë was the first to arrive, which, as Beatrice was to learn, was the norm for double basses. Even if parking was not likely to be a problem, they had to unpack their monstrous gear in the music room, while there was still space before other players arrived.

"What are you doing, Zoë?" Beatrice asked, "moving all my things around?"

"I really need to be right up against the piano," Zoë explained, "sorry if it upsets your plans. In the crook of a grand, or against the bass side of an upright. It helps the intonation."

Beatrice had no time to argue before the doorbell rang, and the cellist, viola and violin arrived in quick succession.

Having tuned, they awaited Araminta, leading, and Beatrice, central to the ensemble on her piano, to co-ordinate their nods, and launched into the first chord.

"No, no, stop!" shouted Araminta, "wait for me to reach the top note of my spread chord. *I'll* nod, you listen... now you know what to expect on the violin, let's try again."

After a few attempts, Araminta was satisfied.

"Is this how it's going to be?" asked Donald in irritation, "stopping half a dozen times at each barline?"

"This is nothing," Zoë reassured him, "I was at a double bass summer school, put my name down for a tutorial with one of the top international players, said I wanted general hints and tips for The Trout, – there's a horrid bit in one of the Variations – and he spent the whole hour, the whole hour, on the first note, the note we're practising now: the attack, where to change bow, how to vary the volume and vibrato as I hold the note for ten bars, you wouldn't believe. *And* I never got any help with my Variation, which is what I really wanted out of the tutorial."

"All right," ventured Charles, "let's play the movement through, warts and all, without stopping if possible, then we'll get a feel."

"Yes," said Beatrice with relief. She knew that a quarter hour of Schubert's music would act as a balm, working its soothing magic on everybody. Donald especially noticed in the development following the long opening repeat how, during his repeated-note passages, he was suddenly enfolded in a warm cocoon of sound which seemed to come from behind him. He enjoyed it, thinking it was probably a chance resonant echo in Beatrice's music room. On the other players too, Schubert's music exerted its calming effect, as they successfully completed the movement.

"Next movement?" asked Charles, the mood now easier. "Araminta, Beatrice, hm, violin or piano, who's meant to call the shots?"

"There's no leader," said Araminta. "We're five different instruments, we're all soloists, we each have tunes…"

"In that case," Charles responded, "I say, next movement please, the slow movement."

"And then I'll make the coffee," said Beatrice.

The slow movement started to give momentary hints of how the piece might sound after more study and rehearsals.

Paradoxically, however, instead of refreshing their attention, the coffee break merely broke their concentration. The Scherzo was rubbish, and the next movement, variations on the Trout theme, was shaky until the last variation (for cello), when Donald again felt the warm cocoon of sound. He found it a supremely comforting feeling. At the end of his variation, something made him look round, and he noticed Zoë looking softly at him.

"Was that all you?" he asked in surprise.

"Yes," she smiled. "Remember, I'm a cellist too, I know what they want and like." She winked.

Coughing loudly to draw attention, Beatrice said, "Yes I know there's a pause written on the barline, but the movement isn't finished yet. Please! We still have the allegretto recapitulation of the main theme, for goodness sake! I've got offbeat triplets to worry about in the piano part, and they have to mesh with Araminta's tempo before I even know what that's going to be!"

After that outburst, this allegretto recapitulation proceeded with a dry formal correctness, despite Charles's efforts to inject some lilt and life into the few notes he had to play, all double-stopped and almost all offbeat.

Araminta and Beatrice looked at each other telepathically.

"Right then," said Beatrice, "I know we haven't played the Finale movement, but we've done all right for a first meeting. Let's call a halt now, before we get fractious, and let's make a date for our next meeting."

As they assembled for their next rehearsal, Araminta asked, "Did you all get Zoë's email? Saying the concert hall she'd organised had shut indefinitely for urgent repairs? Well I've had a piece of good luck, got the phone call just before I set out to come here. We can have the hall at the County School for Girls the exact same night. How did I get it? Oh, I have some violin pupils there, so they know me. The piano? Oh, it's first-rate, nothing but the best there, it's a top day school."

"So, ventured Donald, "we might have some parents in the audience? Seriously knowledgeable people?"

"*Every* audience deserves to be treated as seriously knowledgeable," said Beatrice censoriously. "They can tell subconsciously if we performers are short-changing them."

Zoë was at last able to break in, to thank Araminta. After a collective drawing of breath, they started to tune up. Having, at their previous rehearsal, not reached the Finale movement, they agreed to start with it now, while they were still fresh.

"Are we doing the long repeat in this Finale?" Charles asked.

"Yes, you have to, I think, for balance," said Beatrice, more mildly now.

"Good," said Zoë, "we need to do every possible repeat, to extend the recital to a decent length of time."

"Oh, shame," said Charles, "there's a mini-repeat starting eight or twelve or so bars from the beginning, and I remember to go back correctly first time through, but come the long repeat and when we get to this mini-repeat, I go back to the start of the movement and not to, er," (he looked at his part), "er, *ten* bars after the start, where the mini-repeat really goes back to. It catches me out every time."

"Well, not at the concert please," said Araminta. "And, Charles, do remember please, the second half, after the long repeat, has exactly the same structure with the mini-repeat in exactly the same, well, the corresponding, place."

As they had broken the ice at their first rehearsal, this one went better despite the frequent stops, which were for friendly discussion about matters such as dynamics, which part should be most prominent where, manner of bowing at spots where they needed to co-ordinate, and lengths of held notes.

"It's not *starting* a note together that would make us a great quintet," explained Araminta. "The audience take that for granted - it's *stopping* together, that's what marks out a good ensemble, and if we can end our notes at the ends of phrases in the *same way*, firm, or tailing off, or full value if it's a long note, or whatever it demands, *that'll* make us a top quintet."

While concentrating hard on listening to each other, following Araminta's admonitory pep talk, they enjoyed the last movement, letting Schubert's music speak for itself. They began to think they might reach a standard worth hearing by the time of their concert, even though Donald could hear Zoë cursing herself under her breath for not having adequately practised her awkward arpeggio passages.

When they broke for coffee, Donald assured Zoë that her arpeggios sounded fine.

"But they modulate into all sorts of keys. And arpeggios aren't the doddle on the bass that they are on the cello. Mind you, I shouldn't complain, arpeggios in minor thirds..."

"Like those triplets in the first movement?"

"...yes, those, they're easier on the bass."

"Oh *well* then! *Now* you tell me!" Donald teased. "But more seriously, how did you go about finding your bass? I don't think my local dealer-repairer has any basses at all."

"Too right, bass dealers are few and far between. I had to travel to Hertfordshire to find a place with a good selection, this was when I'd outgrown my student plywood bass. Oh, there were, what, maybe twenty basses in my price range all lined up ready for my visit, and very depressing it was. Some were just too big for me..."

"What, they're not a standard size?"

"Like heck they're not!" she snorted. "Those that were a manageable size and suitable shape, they sounded tired and dull, and I thought, oh dear, why did I take up this thankless instrument, until I got to the very last one. It practically jumped into my lap and sang 'Buy me, buy me'. Oh, and I know what you're thinking, it's not by Matthew Hardie, it's German."

By this time, Beatrice was back at the piano, plinking a tuning A. Donald and Zoë suddenly realised they'd been in their own little world throughout the coffee break.

"We need to concentrate on the Scherzo, and the Theme & Variations," announced Araminta. "At our first play-through..."

"Yes, we know, you don't need to labour the point," interrupted Charles. "Let's get on."

The Scherzo went well with a light humour, and near the end of the repeated second section, Donald and Zoë noticed they had four rhythmic low E's in unison, while nobody else was playing. This came up three times in the movement - twice because of the repeat, then, after the trio section, once more as the "da capo". This became their trade mark joke, as they would always turn towards each other, grinning, at this point.

The Theme & Variations start with the four (all different) stringed instruments, without piano, playing the 'Trout' theme from the song which had been a smash-hit composition by Schubert shortly before he was commissioned to write this quintet. The string players were shocked, as they struggled with their intonation, how reliant they had become on the piano for checking their pitch.

As they moved on to the Variations, each player asked for 'their' Variation to be taken at a slower tempo, Zoë even trying to claim that Variation IV contained the four hardest bars in the entire bass literature.

"But I'm playing exactly the same!" said Donald, "so don't worry, I'll look after you," - at which, Zoë stuck her tongue out at him.

As they had a couple of rehearsals in hand before the concert, Beatrice, sensing they were becoming slightly stale, deliberately surprised them by producing two other quintet compositions at their next meeting.

"What's this?" asked Araminta.

"Change of scenery," explained Beatrice. "Do us good. Bet you didn't know there was a whole literature for this combination!"

"Oh, I knew there was a handful," said Charles, perfectly matter-of-factly, "maybe ten or twelve pieces, is it?"

"Charles, I should really learn never to underestimate your erudition. The two I've brought are by Hummel and by ...Ralph Vaughan Williams."

The Hummel turned out to be in straightforward late-baroque style, which they were able to sight-read all the way through to the end, to near-performance standard, only once or twice having to stop to regroup.

"Well, we've all deserved our coffee now!" said Beatrice, as she stepped away from her piano.

While Beatrice was busy in the kitchen, the others, by unspoken agreement, got out their Schubert parts and played the strings-only Theme, again and again, until they were satisfied.

"Bravo!" shouted Beatrice, reappearing with a tray of coffee and biscuits.

Afterwards, there was time to tackle only the first movement of the Vaughan Williams. This turned out to be extremely tricky to fit together, although moments of Brahms-like beauty did come through.

"It says on the piano part that he withdrew this piece and it's only posthumously that it was published, when his second wife decided to release it. Must try it properly some time. So, same time next week, here at mine, for our last 'Trout' rehearsal."

Beatrice's intuition was proved correct at the next rehearsal, where 'The Trout' was played with a renewed freshness.

At the pre-performance playthrough at the girls' school, in the trio section of the Scherzo, Zoë and Donald both managed to go back to the wrong repeat mark, a mistake neither of them had ever made before. Then, in the Finale, Charles went back to the wrong place as he said he often did, but had never before done in this ensemble.

"Well," said Beatrice, "you've got those mistakes out of your systems now. You're cured. The performance should be fine and..."

A pupil burst in and rushed straight to Araminta. "Miss, miss," she said, "I thought it must be you I heard rehearsing. Oh thank you so much for your advice on chamber playing."

"And what was that, Hermione?"

"If there's a difficult bar I can't play, I must skip notes to make sure I start the next bar in time. Our quartet is so much better now – we can get all the way to the end of a piece together and see how it's meant to go."

"Good girl. Are you coming to the performance tonight?"

"Oh yes, Miss, and lots of my family. The headmistress announced it at assembly, and said what a good cause it was in aid of." The girl then scampered out.

Sure enough, in the evening, the hall was well filled, exceeding Zoë's rather modest hopes for her charity. The headmistress herself said a few well-chosen words of introduction and welcome.

Right from the start, the performance had a happy feel, Zoë in particular smiling to herself as she played her first ten-bars-long note exactly as she had been tutored to do at her bass summer school all those years ago – and suddenly it all made perfect sense. As Beatrice had predicted, there were no mistakes around the repeats, and the whole performance had a sparkling originality. The audience were warmly appreciative.

"Dare we do an encore?" asked Donald.

"Certainly not," ruled Araminta. "Quit while we're ahead. Luck's been on our side tonight; let's keep it that way."

8. *Schubert Op163*

As they returned on a high to their allocated staff room, to put away their instruments before mingling with the audience, Donald asked if they would consider performing the Schubert two-cello quintet.

"What, I switch to cello?" asked Zoë, "Yes, all right, if I get to play Second Cello."

"Oh, yes, please," answered Donald, "You take Second, anything you want, as long as we can carry on working together."

"Is that why you want to do this?" asked Beatrice in amazement, "I saw you working well together – *very* well together, in The Trout, but I'd no idea…"

"Don't embarrass him!" admonished Charles, "Really that was very indelicate, very un-Beatrice-like even. Anyway, *my* answer is, I'd love to perform the Quintet. What's *your* answer? Donald *is* asking us *all*."

Beatrice nodded briefly.

Araminta was amused by her colleagues taking such an initiative without even consulting her as Leader first. On reflection, she realised she was proud too. She had developed her quartet into a team who would each think and act for themselves, but always in the context of the musical whole. Zoë would think and act for herself anyway, it seemed to be part of the innate self-reliance of bass players.

"Do *I* get a say?" asked Araminta, which sent a shock wave through the Green Room, "because, because," hesitating for effect, "...you must realise, it's really one of the top chamber works of all time, and, it, it... would be a *privilege* to lead you."

Back on a high, the five walked jauntily out of the Green Room into the reception room, where the audience were enjoying drinks and nibbles and were looking forward to meeting the musicians.

Afterwards, as they were ready to leave, they pencilled in a rehearsal for the Schubert 2-cello Quintet.

"Donald, where will we be playing it?"

"Well, I still don't really know my way round the music scene here, have you any ideas please?"

"Oh, leave it to me," volunteered Zoë, "I've got various contacts, probably easier for me than for you or Charles or even Beatrice. And I owe Araminta one, for getting us into this school tonight."

Zoë quite quickly secured a recital date for the Schubert 2-cello Quintet. This was for some months ahead, at a residential adult short-course music college, filling a cancellation in its recital series. One of Zoë's friends had performed in this series, and had mentioned to Zoë how the concert was followed by splendid tea and cakes for the audience. Here too, it was customary for the performers to join in and mingle, as the audience (all active musicians at whatever level) genuinely enjoyed meeting the performers afterwards, either for general chat or for more specific discussion about the piece. It was partly this, that had made Zoë approach the college in the first place, to offer this recital.

Although all five were fully committed to the recital, the arguments started almost at once.

Which edition to use? Araminta favoured the most scholarly edition, which Donald decried as having totally impractical page turns. Charles sided with Donald, on the grounds that scholarly accuracy was unattainable, the original manuscript having been discarded when the piece originally flopped, with a score having to be reconstructed later. Araminta countered that the most practical editions tended also to have the most editorially-added spurious phrasing and dynamic markings. An uneasy truce was reached, by which Araminta's favoured edition would be taken as authentic and the other players would amend their own parts accordingly, while she would add into her part the rehearsal letters used in the other editions.

Charles raised a query about the second repeat in the Scherzo movement. Although this is the same in all editions, he suggested that the repeat marking at the end of the second half should have been printed 26 bars earlier, such that the thereby excluded fortissimo passage would instead be heard only on the second and last times. Araminta agreed he might be right, even that the 26 bars in question might have been intended to be heard only as a coda after the 'Da Capo,' but ruled that their forthcoming performance was not the place to try out musicological speculations, however well founded.

Then an argument flared up about their rehearsal timetable. As a quartet, they had fallen into a pattern (of sorts) which suited all their diaries, but with Zoë's new job in IT with a heavy schedule of visiting clients over a wide area, it became a nightmare to pencil in even a monthly rehearsal. They agreed to 'sectional' meetings, whereby Araminta and Beatrice as the violins would agree to rehearse together at a mutually convenient date, while Donald and Zoë as the cellos would likewise rehearse when they had simultaneous free time, and Charles as lone viola would join either of those pairs when he could.

Zoë and Donald concentrated on their exposed unison B-major passages about a hundred bars into the Scherzo movement. Having cracked those, which they eventually did by using the same fingering and shifting, they turned to the lyrical passages in thirds on their higher register about sixty bars into the first movement.

On the occasions that Charles could join them, they looked first at the crudely rustic rumbustious opening of the Scherzo in three-four time. They could not make musical sense of how it immediately followed the deeply introspective Adagio movement, the jewel of the entire piece.

Then, Charles had an insight. "Well, we *won't* play it with leaden peasant boots, all rough fortissimo double stops on the bottom strings. We play it gently, nothing above mezzo-forte at most, we don't dig our bows in, oh yes, we stay rhythmic, but not heavy metal. And... we think it in two-bar phrases..."

"Like it was in six-eight?" asked Donald.

"Exactly. Now let's try. The violins have never liked our clompy accompaniment."

The three of them tried Charles's new softer 6/8 interpretation, and it all made sense.

"I think you've really cracked it, Charles," said Zoë admiringly. "Beatrice and Araminta will be delighted when they join us."

"There's something else, while I think about it," said Charles, seizing the moment. He flapped the pages of his part. "Ah yes, here in the first movement. Look at your pizzicato accompaniment - in this edition, do you have any of the other parts cued in hereabouts? No, I thought probably not. Well, it won't be at all obvious from your part where the phrases end, and where a new instrument takes over. You need to make a note of the places this happens, and get them each to nod you in when they're starting a solo. Actually you cellos start, it's about bar 60, and you'll need to nod to *me* to pizzicato on the first beat, as the violins have off-beat quavers they need to fit in together. Oh, yes, when I've been in with Araminta and Beatrice, they've spent hours on it."

The cellists tried this.

"Good," resumed Charles. "When you two finish your tune here, it's the other way round. Araminta will nod *you* Zoë, as you start the on-beat plucking same as I'd been doing for you. And you need to be decisive about it, as Donald and I have offbeat triplets to fit in together – oh it's amazingly clever writing."

They tried this passage, Charles humming a violin line.

"Even if they forget," explained Charles, "whoever's meant to be nodding their beat to you, at least at that moment, you'll be looking at the right person, and you've a sporting chance of plucking your notes *with* their music. Oh yes it matters. I wish *I* played the cello sometimes, that resonant pizzicato, much more noble than anything a viola can do, but you pay a price of course, you always do in music, you *must* be spot-on in time and in tune with whoever has the tune, no second chances with pizzicato."

Zoë took this to heart and made careful notes as to who led where, making her feel more confident about these corners. This focussed her mind onto her main anxiety, the slow movement. Not just the pizzicati here too, which would make or mar the exposition, but also, on the return to four sharps, her running demisemiquavers accompaniment with way-out accidentals. All the cellists in the audience would know this movement and would be watching her.

Realising that the few full rehearsals they'd been able to schedule would be quite insufficient, Zoë called round all the recreational string quartets she'd ever been connected with, to gatecrash them to play the Quintet. Unknown to Zoë at the time, some of the quartets took this so seriously that they had pre-rehearsals before their date with her!

With this varied experience of so many different quartets, Zoë acquired an instinct which allowed her to stay latched onto the leader, whatever the vagaries of the leader's interpretation of her offbeat semiquaver embellishments to the middle parts. Not that Araminta's playing would ever be subject to vagaries, but the slightest artistic flexibility taken by the leader, maybe to cover hesitancy by the second-violin's and viola's on-beat quavers, could play havoc with the cross-syncopated ensemble.

Now, with her newly acquired instinct, backed up by extensive annotations she had pencilled on her part indicating the rhythms of the first violin's theme, Zoë felt equipped to provide a reliable underpinning to the ensemble whatever the others played, within reason.

Back when they were playing quartets, Araminta had held her tongue when, as part of tuning up, Donald always made a big play of tuning his open C to the viola C. Then, when they were rehearsing The Trout, Zoë took the lead by asking Charles on piano to sound low G, then tuning to it alongside Donald; she was always joking how her top string, in true unison with the cello's third string, was her sole connection to the rest of the ensemble.

Now that they were rehearsing Schubert's Great C-major 2-cello Quintet, Donald was back in his element, fixating on the open Cs. This time, Araminta had to admit, especially given the predominant key of the piece, that three well-tuned Cs provided a fine sonorous foundation to the two violins.

Their five minds concentrated by the limited number of full rehearsals, the likelihood (first appreciated by Zoë) gnawed at them that, at such a venue, the audience would all know the work well and most of them would have played it, if not in public, then certainly recreationally. Nothing less than total effortless command of the work would do.

Because of various external circumstances, even some of their limited full rehearsals had to be cancelled, or run with just four players. Charles's A&E experience at doing the best in minimum time came to the fore, and he suggested, as he had earlier done with the two cellists, that they concentrate on working on the 'corners' in the music, making notes in their parts as to which one of them was 'leading' the music at each of these.

"You can practise your parts by yourselves until you're note-perfect," explained Charles, almost apologetically at stating the obvious, "but you can't practise ensemble by yourself."

With the inadequate ensemble practice time left for the quintet, Zoë was grateful for the indulgence of her friendly quartets who had given her exactly the ensemble practice recommended by Charles.

9. Performance

The day of the concert dawned. The plan was for an early light lunch together at the college, and then an hour or so run-through, leaving time to relax before the performance.

After all the arguments, the cancelled rehearsals and the many changes of arrangements, Araminta, having arrived first, could not contain her relief when all four of her colleagues turned up on time.

As the five took their places and tuned their instruments, they appreciated how well the dais had been laid out for them, but noticed some annoying shadows from the spotlights. Valuable time passed while an assistant climbed onto the dais with a stepladder to adjust the lights.

Their minds focussed by the shortage of time, they took direction from Araminta without query or backchat. Playing in 'workmanlike' rather than 'beautiful' mode, they successfully topped and tailed each movement in turn, as well as covering the more significant tempo and mood changes. They had just started the last movement and were trying to settle on an Allegretto tempo which would suit the acoustic of the hall, when the same assistant burst in.

"I'm really sorry to interrupt," he said, "but we've never had such a crowd. They're overflowing the corridors and we'll have to let them in to the hall. Yes, *now*, it's a public safety issue."

"Oh," said Charles, "my wife is coming. She's looking round the town just now, but I hope she gets in, if it's going to be as full as that!"

"Shall I put out a call for her?" asked the assistant, "or, for all of you, shall I take names of your people to give them priority?"

"No, no," said Charles, "my wife would be tremendously embarrassed." The others also declined this offer.

All five then reluctantly took up their instruments and started to make their way off. Zoë's shoe caught on the foot of a music stand and, in steadying herself, she accidentally let go of her cello. The noise was sickening. On gingerly picking up her cello, she saw the bridge was down but there seemed to be no other damage, apart from deep scratches made by the (now loose-swinging) tailpiece.

"That was awful, but you were lucky," said Donald, once they were all back in the green room. "The fingerboard could have come off, or the soundpost could have fallen when the pressure on it was released."

Zoë checked the soundpost and started the laborious task of placing the bridge, checking its angle, tightening each string just slightly, rechecking the bridge position and angle, tightening each string, adjusting the bridge position...

"Oh *no!!*" wailed Zoë, "I've broken the bridge!"

"You *can't* have," said Donald unhelpfully. "Oh, I see, a Belgian bridge, hm, very slender legs, oh dear."

"I'll find someone," said Beatrice, getting up. "Oh my, you can see the car park from here, gosh it's filling up."

Soon, Beatrice returned with the college Principal, who was on hand anyway to say a few words of welcome and introduction at the recital.

He took in the situation at a glance: Zoë curled up and sobbing quietly, Donald ineffectually trying to console her, Charles helplessly examining the broken bridge, and Araminta with the look of a general whose plans have been wrecked by her allies.

"Oh, but this is all soluble," said the college Principal in a reassuring calm voice. "We have an Instrument Hire scheme on the premises, it loans out top-quality instruments to deserving young players, while they get started on their careers. I'll see if the Director has a spare cello ready to go out. Please don't worry, this recital *will* be able to go ahead, whatever."

As he left, Zoë somewhat recovered her composure, until she noticed, through the door that the Principal had accidentally left slightly ajar, that helpers were carrying extra seats into the auditorium.

The other four started to play the Quintet from memory, and indeed, only those four are playing for the first ten bars. When they reached her entry at bar 11, Zoë started to feel sick, not helped by the sight of the car park continuing to fill up.

A few minutes later, the Director of the Instrument Hire scheme came in. "You're in luck. There's a very good cello, I would have brought it in for you but the crowd's too thick, so I had to go in the hall through a back door and put it direct on the stage. I've tuned it using my phone app, best I could do with the audience already in there taking their seats. Do you need a bow..? Ah, you're all right. Well, I must be off. Good luck!"

Perform this mighty piece on a cello she'd never even touched before? Zoë wondered why she'd ever let herself be talked into this project.

The Principal then fought his way through the press of people back into the green room, and invited the quintet to take their places on stage. Helpers cleared a way through the throng. Zoë caught sight of some of the players from the quartets she'd imposed upon. She couldn't let them down now.

The Principal said a few words of introduction, which passed Zoë by as she tried to guess, by feel, how her substitute cello would react. When they all tuned, she had her first clue. It responded easily, but without the bright carrying tone of her usual cello.

She pretended to heed Araminta's signal to start, but out of politeness only, as she had ten bars' rest.

When she did start, in Bar 11, with two breves of D, the others looked round, unable to hear her usual strong tone and uncertain whether she was actually playing. This went on for bar after bar, until nearly fifty bars in, she was playing in a lower octave than the others and they could at last hear for certain that she really was playing. Come the two-cellos melody at Bar 60, her sound blended so well with Donald's that the audience started to realise this was a performance out of the ordinary.

All the corners which Charles had mentioned in the pre-rehearsals went correctly. Zoë wished her pizzicato notes on this cello had been stronger, but they had a resonance which compensated for their lack of edge. The long first movement passed by as if in a dream, topped by an exquisitely phrased closing arpeggio from Araminta.

The five allowed themselves a few moments' breather, before Araminta signalled for Beatrice, as second violin, to lead them into the Adagio movement. Zoë worried whether she could muster the strength for her crucial pace-determining pizzicato notes. But the others were instinctively playing half-a-notch quieter. Zoë's plucked notes now revealed themselves as more than rhythmic glue, they were almost a counter-melody. The others appreciated her plucked notes in this movement for a different reason, namely their unerring regularity of beat, a benefit of Zoë's double-bass experience.

At the exquisite modulation in the slow movement back from 4 flats to 4 sharps, which the quintet had spent hours perfecting, Zoë had learned a way to pitch her first note of the interrupted cadence reliably: she would lightly touch the open G string, just enough for her ear to get an accurate "fix" on the pitch, allowing her, regardless of any slight intonation wobbles leading to this moment, to accurately place the half-position G-sharp root of the chord.

The performance had now reached this point, and she was about to touch the open string to gauge its pitch, when she realised that the packed auditorium was in absolute silence. Her secret sound, even on this non-penetrating cello, would carry and be heard. The audience's total undivided attention was on the performance.

They would easily have heard a pin drop, let alone have heard an experimental plinking of an open string to get a fix on the pitch.

Nothing for it but to hope she could find half-position accurately.

She did, and the performance took a new dimension. The others, in top-concentration mode, were more disciplined in their rhythms and the ensemble blossomed. Zoë's notorious running-demisemiquavers passage, on this softer cello, no longer sounded like a silver contrast thread on a dark cloth, but became the unobtrusive heartbeat integrating the ensemble. Beatrice and Donald were reminded of their Schubert piano trio performance, where it seemed it wasn't until the actual performance that they had fully tapped into the essence of the music. Araminta and Zoë knew nothing of that event, but for themselves felt their parts had interlocked with a logic that had previously eluded them.

On the final recapitulation of that movement, the first violin has to join in with plucked notes accompanying her own tune, very awkward to fit in without losing the rhythm. But with Zoë's quieter pizzicato, Araminta found she could balance the volume without stress, allowing her to give her trade-mark calm but totally-in-control performance.

The five had previously agreed to have a re-tune at the end of the slow movement, but when they finished the last chord, the audience remained stock-still and silent. Tuning now would kill the atmosphere the five had managed to create, and, by gestures, they each indicated they would forego tuning-up.

But this only hastened their next problem, the major one of playing the remaining two movements as if they were on the same exalted level of inspiration as the first two. Charles's ideas had better be right about playing the Scherzo softly and in two-bar phrases to avoid the over-violent change of mood that the score seemed to specify.

"Sorry, Schubert," Charles was thinking to himself, "this might not be what you actually had in mind, but we have to do it for your audience. For their sakes, we can't crash them out of that magical atmosphere."

They did play it more tenderly than the rustic style implied by the markings and dynamics, and Zoë's gentler tone on this cello made the low-strings chords much more acceptable.

The central Trio section, Andante Sostenuto in unrelated key, time signature and tempo, represent a tranquil contrast to the rustic Scherzo. But now, when the performance reached this point, the only way the five could establish a contrast was to play the Trio section even more hauntingly than they had ever done in rehearsal. In the event, Zoë's substitute cello could have been made for the purpose, blending as one with Charles's tone as they played in octaves. When the other three joined in after a few bars' rest, the harmonies were superficially beautiful, but the Trio as a whole offered merely empty desolation. *Now* the five understood why the Scherzo had to be lively, and they let their hair down in its recapitulation.

The audience also relaxed, with minor fidgeting, coughing and paper rustling at the end of this movement.

Now the Finale. Thoroughly warmed up, completely without nerves, the five started at a livelier tempo than they intended, but maintained good ensemble until the Più Allegro, when it became slightly ragged in the excitement.

The final Più Presto was taken at frankly reckless speed, with Araminta and Zoë pushing each other through their interlocked ornamented turns until Zoë's on-the-beat notes formed a foundation for a few bars of wild syncopations leading to the exhilarating chase to the last three chords. Though strong, they are far from being triumphal, they are blank and forlorn.

On reaching these final chords, the five performers recovered their discipline, playing these chords exactly as agreed in rehearsal: They gave the last D-flat grace note a full crotchet's-worth of time and the C-semibreve fermata a further five crotchets'-worth exactly. And, at the very end, they allowed the open Cs to continue to ring after the bows were lifted.

The effect was as planned. The music had gone through all the moods from sublime to exciting to ... empty hopeless finality.

After several seconds, someone tentatively started to clap. Someone else joined it, and in moments the recital hall was alive with cheering and stamping.

When they were eventually able to cease acknowledging the applause, Donald asked in wonderment, "Were we really as good as that?"

10. Finale

Taking their instruments, they stepped down from the dais and an assistant ushered them across the hall back into the Green Room. They were just drawing breath when there was a knock at the door, and the Principal appeared, accompanied by a lady.

"This is the Secretary of the Matthew Hardie Society," explained the Principal. "She is very keen to talk to you and see your instruments – as I understand three of them are by Matthew Hardie, at least that's what I put in the programme and in the advance publicity. Well, I'll leave you now; if you need me, I'll be around, talking to the audience. They were very appreciative. 'Bye for now."

"I've been looking forward to this," said the lady when he left. "Our Society is all about studying Matthew Hardie's life and work, and following up where his instruments are now. And now I get to see three in one visit!"

"So how did you get interested?" asked Beatrice.

"It's in the family mythology," answered the lady. "One of my forebears had a Matthew Hardie, and somehow that fact sparked my interest. So, you actually call yourselves the Hardie Quartet, don't you, plus your guest cellist" (she squinted at the programme for the names), "er, Zoë. Oh, your names," she continued conversationally, "What a coincidence, I knew a Charles once, same surname as you, but he played the violin not the viola. Anyway, I'm sorry if all of this has cut across your plans for this afternoon. I did email the Hardie Quartet but it must have got lost."

"Oh, are you Katrina Young?" asked Charles. "We did get your message but it, um, it wasn't convenient at the time."

Araminta remembered Charles's confusion when he originally mentioned that e-mail. To rescue him, she turned the conversation back and said, "If it helps your researches, the dealer when I bought this violin could trace its history back to 1815."

The others pricked up their ears; even Donald and Zoë unclinched themselves. Araminta had never told them this before.

"Oh, this an amazing breakthrough," said Katrina gratefully, pulling out a camera and a notebook from her bag. "Tell me more please, I'm ready."

Trying not to be noticed, Charles glanced at her eyes, remembering the unusual dark blue eyes of 'his' Katrina. Oh no, oh God, please not...

Araminta started to tell Katrina: "Well, in 1815, so the dealer told me, it was bought at auction for his fiddler by Lord Shetland..."

"But that's exactly him! He was my great-something-grandfather!"

Katrina Shetland. It was really her. Charles shook uncontrollably.

At this instant, there was a knock at the door and Charles's wife was shown in by an assistant.

"Hello, my dear," said Charles, taking deep breaths in an attempt to regain some composure. "This is the Secretary of the Matthew Hardie Society. She..."

"Charles, dear, you're trembling. You look as if you'd seen a ghost."

"Yes dear. Well, not a ghost. But still a shock. It's a most unexpected reunion. We, er, knew each other at university, but that was all over before I met you, so I never mentioned..."

"So," his wife gently asked him, "is this Katrina?"

"How do you know *that?!* I never mentioned..."

"Ah," she smiled. Looking now at Katrina, she added, "I've always known. He's always muttering your name in his sleep." Turning back to her husband, she said, "Charles dear, you're in no fit state. Go sit in the Principal's office and calm down over a cup of tea, then go and circulate among your admiring public. They're asking among themselves why you haven't appeared yet."

"Yes dear," he said, grateful for his wife's deft defusing of the situation. She would do well in an A&E department, he thought admiringly as he left the room.

When the door was safely shut, Araminta broke the awkward silence. "I'm sorry, Katrina, I didn't mean to drop you in all this."

"Don't worry, you couldn't possibly have known," said Katrina, continuing, for Charles's wife's benefit, "We were friends at university – we played together in one of the lesser orchestras – but there was never anything, and I really don't how he could ever have imagined there was. Didn't know he played viola though; silly man, they were crying out for violas even in the top orchestra."

"Can we get back to the instruments please?" interjected Beatrice. "If we're meant to mingle with the audience, we should really do that now, and one of us stay behind here, with you."

"That should obviously be me," offered Charles's wife, "as long as you're happy for me to handle your instruments if Katrina needs. Oh yes, I'm absolutely fine, now I know the full background."

This being agreed, Katrina asked for the violins and viola to be laid side-by-side and held in position. Taking her camera, she pointed out the common features, the scrolls, the varnish.

As she looked more closely at the grain, she asked, "Can you put them end-to-end... I can't believe... the fronts, the bellies, the tables, whatever you want to call them, they match, all three from the same log..."

She took more photos and continued, "We know he bought up second-hand wood, and we also know – oh, it's all in his account books – yes, they became available in the public bankruptcy archives, they're digitised on our website now – he got occasional commissions for quartets of instruments."

"Ah, but the cellos aren't Hardies," Charles's wife pointed out.

"That's just what bugs me," said Katrina, "the two cellos look so amazingly similar to these three, which I *do* think *are* a set."

"Yes, but Donald's been to our house for rehearsals," said Charles's wife, "and he seems to have this chip on his shoulder about his cello *not* being a Hardie but by, can't remember, some other name."

"Well let's have a look," said Katrina, "Donald's was slightly the shinier cello of the two. This one." Shining the torch on her phone through the f-hole, she exclaimed, "Joseph Meall! Joseph Meall indeed! What a con-man! The court records make interesting reading, I can tell you... Now, what about the chisel marks inside, yes, Donald's cello is definitely part of this set all made by Hardie. My bet is, some other poor cellist out there is under the illusion he possesses a Hardie, when all he really possesses is the label *taken out of* this masterpiece."

There was a knock at the door. The lady who came in said, "Oh, hello, sorry to interrupt, when I saw Zoë come out, I thought... oh, who am *I*? Of course, sorry, I'm the Director of our Instrument Hire Library. I've come to take Zoë's loan cello back to our strongroom. Yes, didn't you know? When Zoë damaged her cello just before coming on, she had to borrow one of ours. There wasn't any time for her to come over and pick and choose, I just had to find anything that was immediately ready to play."

"Well, it certainly blended well," said Katrina, "but the other four instruments, it's astonishing, I think what I've just discovered is that what we have here is none other than a quartet of instruments made, *as a set,* by Matthew Hardie..."

"Oh, this is exciting. I must tell the Principal!" said the Director, rushing out of the room.

"...but, oh never mind then," Katrina's voice tailed off. She fell silent and started to examine Zoë's hire-scheme cello. She took some photographs, then kneeled on the floor, shone her torch and put her little mirror into the f-hole. Throughout her increasing perplexity, she carried on working, then consulted her tablet, and was deep in thought when Charles's wife spoke: "My word, you're so purposeful, you're so determined. I can see why my Charles so fancied you."

"Yes, well *I* never fancied *him*, and I'm in a more important quandary than that, right now. The label in Zoë's loan cello, *'Rebuilt by David Stirrat'*. Now what's all that about? And the studs and repairs inside, it was well smashed up, this cello, long ago. And yet the grain's an even closer match to your Charles's viola than Donald's cello is. I must just check something," and she returned to perusing her tablet. She moved from page to page.

Suddenly, punching the air in triumph, she shouted **"*Yes!*"**, to the astonishment of an assistant who was just coming in at that moment.

"You're wanted in the main foyer," said the assistant, "Yes, urgently, now! I'll lock up. Yes, the audience are still there in the foyer having their tea and cakes; hardly anyone's gone home."

Charles's wife and Katrina arrived just in time to hear the Principal tapping a spoon against a teacup for silence. He cleared his throat.

"Ladies and gentlemen! Here is an important announcement."

"Yes!" shouted Donald, jumping up, "Zoë and I are engaged!"

There was applause and cheering. The Principal waited until it died down.

"Well, I can't top that," he said, "and we all wish Donald and Zoë a long and happy life together. But may I say how privileged we have been to hear such an extraordinary performance this afternoon. You won't realise just how extraordinary. An astonishing historical discovery has just been made, in the last few minutes. In the audience this afternoon we were honoured to have Mrs Katrina Young, the Secretary of the Matthew Hardie Society – and I see she's just joined us here now. She has made this discovery, and for fear of being interrupted by other engagement announcements" [there was polite laughter], "I will merely reveal that what you heard today was a quartet of four instruments made by Matthew Hardie as a set, which by a chain of amazing coincidences has been re-united, *and the players never knew,* until now. So I'll step aside and let Mrs Young, as the expert, describe the whole thing in her own words, in her own way."

Taken by surprise and unprepared, Katrina shuffled through the crowd to stand alongside the Principal.

"It's exactly as the Principal here has said," Katrina started. Hesitating, she continued, "But you don't want the technical details of how I was able to work all this out – I can write them up for your house magazine maybe."

The Principal nodded.

"Fine, but what I really want to say is, I made a further discovery, literally the minute I was called back here to join you all. Now, before the performance, I can't remember it being announced that Zoë, yes congratulations on your engagement - Zoë had damaged her own cello, and at the last minute was lent a cello from here without even any chance to try it out before she went on."

There was spontaneous applause.

"Well, I looked at her borrowed cello out of general interest, because the colour and grain are so very similar to the other four. In fact the grain is an even closer match to the upper instruments than is Donald's. All five come from the same log, that was clear from the start. Well, I looked inside Zoë's cello for a label, and it said 'Rebuilt by David Stirrat'. Now that rang a bell in my mind, because he worked in Edinburgh at much the same time as Matthew Hardie."

Warming to her theme, she continued, "So I called up Matthew Hardie's account books – they're digitised on my tablet – and searched for 'Stirrat'. And there it was, in his 1814 ledger."

She picked up her tablet and read out: *"'Received, 3 guineas balance after deposit, from Mr Andrew Darroch, for replacement cello for his eldest daughter Isobel, with front made from remainder of same log as original quartet set. Original cello broken and its tonewood given to David Stirrat of Fleshmarket, no charge, in return for favour rendered.'* Well, I obviously then searched under 'Darroch', and there it was, in 1811, same date as the labels in the violins and viola here, a quartet set of instruments commissioned for his four daughters. If I find anything more about this Andrew Darroch, I'll add it to my article for your house magazine."

"Thank you," said the Principal, "That'll make interesting reading indeed."

Katrina concluded, "Somehow then, this, the original Darroch cello, now rebuilt, fetched up here two centuries later, ready for Zoë in her hour of need."

"So," summed up the Principal, "you're telling us we heard a *quintet* of instruments, including a *second cello,* all from the same log and all commissioned from the same maker by Mr Darroch for his four daughters!"

There was applause, and, by some unspoken communal instinct, everyone moved slowly back to the auditorium.

The players went to the Green Room, which was hastily unlocked for them to collect their instruments. Nobody said a word – they didn't need to; it was obvious what to do. The players slowly returned to the dais.

Aware now that their five instruments were a reunited set, they played the slow movement of the Schubert Quintet as it had never been heard before.

- - - - -